"Your wife may now reveal her face."

Sheikh Sharif Bin Noor Al Nazar waited with bated breath as his new wife's attendants came forward to unhook the elaborate mask that had hidden her face for the duration of the wedding ceremony.

Not even her eyes had been visible.

Sharif couldn't care less what she looked like—he had no intention of consummating this marriage. It was to be in name only for as short amount of time as possible—but if she was at least passably attractive, that would certainly make things easier for him.

The delicate chains and gold medallions of the covering clinked as it was removed and her face was revealed.

The first thing Sharif noted somewhat dispassionately was that he didn't have to worry about her being passably attractive—because she was stunningly beautiful.

The second was more of a visceral reaction. Shock, followed quickly by anger. Because Aaliyah was far from being the stranger he'd expected— was not in fact a stranger.

Not at all. In fact he knew her intimately.

One word resounded in Sharif's head. He wasn't even sure if he uttered it out loud. *"You!"*

The Marchetti Dynasty

They live a superrich lifestyle—but for this dynasty to survive, these brothers need brides!

The Marchetti name is synonymous with luxury— their family business boasts the most opulent brands from fashion to real estate. While the three Marchetti brothers live a superrich existence and have no trouble attracting women, they know little about love and have even less in common, apart from the emotional scars of their dysfunctional relationships with their unscrupulous father—and their resulting bachelor statuses! Now they are going to have to work together to protect their inheritance—and securing the Marchetti dynasty will mean learning that gaining wives and heirs is going to take far more than a little seduction!

Meet the Marchetti brothers and the feisty and resourceful women who tame them in:

Nikos and Maggie's story:
The Maid's Best Kept Secret

Maks and Zoe's story:
The Innocent Behind the Scandal

Sharif and Aaliyah's story:
Bride Behind the Desert Veil

All available now!

Abby Green

—

BRIDE BEHIND THE
DESERT VEIL

HARLEQUIN

PRESENTS

H HARLEQUIN®
PRESENTS®

PLEASE RECYCLE
THIS PRODUCT IS RECYCLABLE

Recycling programs
for this product may
not exist in your area.

ISBN-13: 978-1-335-40354-4

Bride Behind the Desert Veil

Harlequin Enterprises ULC
22 Adelaide St. West, 40th Floor
Toronto, Ontario M5H 4E3, Canada
www.Harlequin.com

Printed in U.S.A.

Irish author **Abby Green** ended a very glamorous career in film and TV—which really consisted of a lot of standing in the rain outside actors' trailers—to pursue her love of romance. After she'd bombarded Harlequin with manuscripts, they kindly accepted one, and an author was born. She lives in Dublin, Ireland, and loves any excuse for distraction. Visit abby-green.com or email abbygreenauthor@gmail.com.

Books by Abby Green

Harlequin Presents

Awakened by the Scarred Italian
The Greek's Unknown Bride

One Night With Consequences

An Innocent, A Seduction, A Secret

The Marchetti Dynasty

The Maid's Best Kept Secret
The Innocent Behind the Scandal

Rival Spanish Brothers

Confessions of a Pregnant Cinderella
Redeemed by His Stolen Bride

Visit the Author Profile page
at Harlequin.com for more titles.

This is for Ellen Walsh. We've been best friends since we were skinny little nippers running around the back fields and cliff ways of Ballybunion. I treasure our friendship and the roots from which it came. Love you lots, always.

PROLOGUE

'YOUR WIFE MAY now reveal her face.'

Sheikh Sharif Bin Noor Al Nazar waited with bated breath as his new wife's attendants came forward to unhook the elaborate face mask that had covered her face for the duration of the wedding ceremony.

Not even her eyes had been visible.

Sharif couldn't care less what she looked like—he had no intention of consummating this marriage; it was to be in name only for as short amount of time as possible—but if she was at least passably attractive that would certainly make things easier for him.

The delicate chains and gold medallions of the face covering clinked as it was removed and her face was revealed.

The first thing Sharif noted somewhat dispassionately was that he didn't have to worry about her being passably attractive—because she was stunningly beautiful.

The second thing was more of a visceral reaction. Shock, followed quickly by anger. Because his new wife, far from being the stranger he'd expected, was not in fact a stranger.

Not at all. In fact he knew her intimately.

One word resounded in Sharif's head. He wasn't even sure if he uttered it out loud. *'You!'*

CHAPTER ONE

Two weeks ago

'YOU'RE SAYING YOU don't even know what your bride-to-be looks like?'

The horrified expression on Nikos Marchetti's face was almost comical. Sharif Marchetti's younger half-brother was on a video call from his home in Ireland, where Sharif could see his wife, Maggie, pregnant again, pottering in the background with their eight-month-old baby son, Daniel, on one arm. For some strange reason Sharif found the domestic scene presented before him... distracting.

Because it was catching at something inside him. A place it shouldn't be catching. Because he found such domesticity utterly alien and unwelcome.

He focused on his brother. 'No, I don't know what she looks like. I know nothing about her and I'm not interested. I'm marrying her because of a diplomatic agreement between Al-Murja and

Taraq that has to be honoured. And,' he tacked on with studied nonchalance, 'because settling down appears to be good for business.'

That was an understatement. Since both his younger half-brothers had recently taken wives—Maks, their youngest brother, had married his wife in a private civil ceremony in London just before Christmas—the Marchetti Group's stock value had gone through the roof.

But Sharif knew it could go even higher, reaching a stability and value that would finally bring him close to achieving all he'd set out to achieve when his father had died. When the old man had finally relinquished his control over the company that had been built off the backs of the fortunes of others. Namely, each one of his three wives—Sharif's mother, and the mothers of Nikos and Maks.

Maggie's face, and Daniel's cherubic one, appeared over Nikos's shoulder. 'Al-Murja and Taraq? An arranged marriage? It all sounds so exotic!'

Sharif wrangled his focus back to the present moment. Nikos was reaching for his son, tucking him competently against his chest while commenting drily to his wife, who had come to perch on his knee, 'Sharif doesn't operate at the level of mere mortals. On this side of the world he's a Marchetti, and merely one of the world's most successsful billionaires, but in his mother's desert home of Al-Murja he's a royal sheikh and even goes by a different name.'

Maggie's big blue eyes opened wide. 'Ooh, Sharif, I never knew that. What's your other name?'

There was a knock on the door of Sharif's office in Manhattan. He welcomed it, not liking how this familiarity was impacting upon him. Over the last few months he and his brothers might have developed more of an affinity than they'd ever had before, but they were still far from being truly functional as a family.

'My car is here. I'll be in touch, Nikos, as soon as I'm back.'

His brother shook his head. 'Why are you doing this again?'

Sharif forced a smile he wasn't feeling. 'Because I'm envious of what you and Maks have, brother. I want to be as happy as you.'

But as Sharif terminated the connection on Nikos's sharp burst of disbelieving laughter, his deep-seated cynicism rubbed against something raw. Something he knew would only be made less raw when he stood over the dismantled pieces of the Marchetti Group and ground his father's legacy to dust.

His conscience pricked as he sat in the back of his chauffeur-driven limousine a few minutes later, thinking of his half-brothers and how they might react if they knew his plans. But he

quashed the feeling. They had no more allegiance
to their father than he had. And, as much as they
might have developed an affinity, he didn't trust
anyone with his plans. Not even them.

When the time came he would tell them and they
would walk away with wealth beyond their means.

What more could they want?

One week ago, Taraq

'Why should I let you take your sister's place for
this marriage?' asked the King.

Aaliyah Binte Rashad Mansour did her best to
stay calm, but she was gritty-eyed from lack of
sleep after the frantic journey she'd just taken from
England back to her desert home in the middle of
the Arabian Peninsula, after an hysterical phone
call from her beloved younger half-sister Samara.

'Because I'm your eldest daughter. Samara is
only nineteen.'

And she was in love with the son of the King's
chief aide.

Liyah's father said nothing more for a moment,
and she pressed on while she had a chance. 'Samara hasn't even met this man you want her to
marry. Clearly they're strangers. What does it
matter if it's me and not her?'

Her sister had told her, *'He just wants a wife.
He doesn't care who that is, as long as it's someone from this family.'*

Her father made an indistinct sound. He wasn't a very tall man. Liyah was almost taller, at five foot ten. She'd always felt that he disapproved of her less than delicate proportions. Among the myriad other things that she'd never understood.

Her mother had been his first wife, and she had died when Liyah was a toddler. Liyah had only the vaguest memories of being rocked, and a lullaby being sung, but she'd long since convinced herself that was just a weak fantasy to make up for the fact that when her father had married again and had his other children, Liyah had been effectively sidelined and forgotten about. Neglected.

The only family member Liyah had ever allowed close was Samara who, since she was tiny, had followed Liyah around like a faithful shadow, crashing through all of Liyah's barriers.

As soon as she'd known Samara was in distress, and why, Liyah hadn't thought twice about coming home and offering herself in her sister's place. But now that she was here in front of her father a sense of panic gripped her.

'Who is he, anyway? And why is he happy to marry a woman he doesn't even know? I thought we'd moved on from arranged marriages.'

'Don't be naive, Aaliyah. The best marriages are still primarily the ones that are arranged for the benefit of two parties—in this instance two neighbouring kingdoms that have a long history of enmity.'

'But it's been years since anything—'

Her father interrupted. 'He's the cousin of the King of Al-Murja and he's honouring a decades-old diplomatic agreement by marrying into this family and providing a dowry. His mother was meant to marry your uncle, but she took off to Europe and married an Italian playboy instead, giving him her dowry. That marriage fell apart and she came home in disgrace with a baby son. She died when he was still young and his father brought him up.'

That story rang a few vague bells in Liyah's head. But her father had stopped pacing and now looked at her. There was a gleam in his dark eyes—very unlike Liyah's green ones.

'His mother ran off to Europe just as you did. Clearly you share her rebellious spirit, Aaliyah.'

Indignation made Liyah's spine tense. 'It's hardly rebellious to want to—'

Her father held up a hand, cutting her off again. 'No, I think this will work very well, actually. Sheikh Sharif Bin Noor Al Nazar controls a vast luxury conglomerate in Europe. He will not stand for a rebellious wife. He is just what you need to learn some control, Aaliyah. To learn respect.'

A million things bubbled in Liyah's blood, chief of which were a very familiar hurt and the need to defend herself, but she forced herself to swallow it all down and ask, 'So does this mean that you'll let me take Samara's place?'

Her father looked at her for a long moment. There wasn't a hint of warmth or approval in his eyes. Just the cool disdain that had become so familiar. Then he said, 'Yes, you will be the one to marry Sheikh Sharif Bin Noor Al Nazar. And you will use this as an opportunity to redeem yourself in the eyes of this family.'

Liyah's relief was tempered with panic at what she'd just done, but she couldn't back out now. Not when Samara's happiness was at stake. She would do anything for her sister.

Her father was turning away from her, clearly done with the conversation, and shock that he could dismiss her so easily after all but handing her over to a complete stranger for the rest of her life made Liyah blurt out, 'Why do you care for me so little, Father?'

He stopped. He faced her again, and for the first time in her life Liyah saw something flicker to life in his eyes. Incredibly. It was only after he spoke that she realised what it was: acute pain.

He said, 'Because your mother was the only woman I loved and you look exactly like her. So every day that you're alive and she isn't is a reminder of what I have lost.'

Yesterday

Sharif saw the falcon first. A peregrine falcon. Mature. He guessed at least ten years old. Magnificent. Feathers reflecting golden tints in the dying rays of the sun. Its grace and seemingly lazy circles in the air didn't fool Sharif. It was looking for prey and would swoop and kill within a split second.

He was about to find his binoculars to have a closer look when he heard the sound of a horse's hooves. One horse.

He shrank back into the shadows of the trees around the natural pool at the oasis where he'd set up camp for the night, en route to the palace at Taraq. His team had gone on ahead. He needed some time alone in the desert. It never failed to ground and recharge him, and he knew the coming weeks would require all of his focus…

A horse and rider thundered into the small but lush oasis, shattering the peace. In an instant Sharif assessed the young man to be an expert horseman, his body moving as one with the horse. The enormous stallion came to an abrupt halt under a twitch of the reins, nostrils flaring, body sheened with a light film of sweat. He'd been ridden hard.

The young man slid off athletically, patting the horse's neck and leading it over to the pool where it drank thirstily. He looped the reins around a nearby tree, tethering the horse.

Sharif wasn't sure why he stayed hidden in the shadows, but some instinct was compelling him to remain hidden for now. He sensed the stranger's desire to be alone. Like him. Also, he presumed the rider would move on once the horse had drunk and rested for a moment.

He couldn't make out the man's—the *boy's* face. He had to be a boy. He was tall, but too slight to be a man. His head and face were covered in a loose turban.

The falcon swooped low at that moment and Sharif saw the rider lift up his right arm. The bird came to rest on a leather arm-guard. So it was a pet falcon. Impressive.

The stranger fed the bird what looked like a piece of meat out of a pouch at his hip and then, with a flick of his arm, let the bird fly off again.

The young man stood at the edge of the pool. A sigh seemed to go through his slender frame. And then he lifted his hands to undo his turban.

Sharif moved to announce himself, but stopped in his tracks when the turban fell away and a riotous mass of dark unruly curls was unleashed, tumbling down a narrow back. *Narrow back. Long hair. Curls.*

It hit Sharif. This wasn't a young man—it was a young woman, and as he watched, struck mute and unable to move, she started to take off all her clothes.

The gallop to the oasis had only taken the smallest edge off Liyah's turmoil—a potent mixture of anger and helplessness. It was the eve of her wedding and she was hopelessly trapped. And she'd put herself in this position for the sake of her sister, which only made her feel even more impotent. It wasn't as if she was being forced into this. She could have ignored her sister's call. Stayed in Europe.

Yet, she couldn't have. She adored her sister— the only family member who had ever shown Liyah love and acceptance. Liyah would do anything to secure Samara's happiness. Even this.

And, after extracting a promise from her father that he wouldn't stand in the way of Samara marrying her sweetheart, Javid, at least Liyah's sacrifice wouldn't be in vain.

But it wasn't even that sacrifice that was uppermost in her mind. She was still reeling from what her father had revealed a week ago. That he'd loved her mother. And that Liyah reminded him of her.

Knowing the reason why she'd always been shunned by her father wasn't exactly a comfort. It only compounded her sense of dislocation. Isolation. Love had done this to her father—made him bitter.

In a way, discovering this had only confirmed her belief that love was not to be trusted. It made you weak and vulnerable.

If anything, she more than most should agree with a marriage based on the sound principles of practicality and necessity. She just hadn't ever figured that she would have to put it into practice. She'd relished the prospect of an independent life. Free to make choices of her own.

Living in Europe for the past couple of years had given her a false sense of freedom. That freedom had been an illusion. Even if she hadn't come back here to take her sister's place, her family's neglect and disapproval would have always cast a long shadow, reminding her of how unlovable she was.

Since her father had mentioned that her husband-to-be was the CEO of a luxury conglomerate, Liyah imagined him to be the sort of individual who gorged himself on rich food, beautiful women and vacuous pleasures.

She didn't want to blight her last days of freedom—*ha!*—by thinking of a future she couldn't change, so she hadn't even bothered to look him up. Which she knew wasn't exactly rational—but then she hadn't been feeling very rational for the last week as the full enormity of what she'd agreed to sank in.

The water of the deep pool looked inviting and cool and she felt hot and constricted. Panicky.

She let the turban that had been wound around her head and face to protect her from the sand drop to the ground. She started to take off her clothes, knowing she was safely alone because no one ever came here. It was too close to the palace to be a stopping point for travellers. And the Sheikh—her future husband—had arrived just before she'd left, with an entourage. Not that she'd hung around to see him.

She undid the buttons on her shirt and it fell down her arms with a soft whoosh. The cooling evening air made her skin prickle. She undid her bra, let that fall too. She opened the button on her soft leather trousers—trousers that her father would never approve of as they were not feminine. Which was precisely why Liyah loved them. Apart from the ease of movement they gave her.

She shimmied them over her hips and then down her legs, stepping out of them. She pulled down her underwear.

Now she was naked.

Her horse whinnied softly. The sky was a dark bruised lavender, filling with stars. A crescent moon was rising. A swell of emotion made her chest tight. Would she ever be back here again? She loved this place. It was where she felt most at peace. Cantering over the sand with her bird high in the sky above her. Wild. Free.

Liyah stepped into the water, still warm after the day's intense heat. It glided over her skin like silk as she walked in up to her waist and then dived deep, where the depths were cooler and darker.

Only when her lungs were about to burst did she kick her way back up and break the surface, sucking in deep gulps of air. It took a second for her ears to clear before she heard a man's voice.

'What the hell were you doing? I was about to rescue you.'

At the sound of the voice Liyah whirled around in the water to face the shore. Shock at the sight of the very tall, broad and dark stranger almost made her sink under the surface again.

His hands were on his hips and he stood in the shallows, the end of his long white robe drifting in the water. He had short, thick dark hair. His jaw was stubbled. But even through her shock Liyah could see that he was breathtakingly handsome. And powerful.

His eyes looked dark too. High cheekbones. A firm mouth. Currently in a disapproving line.

That line of disapproval snapped Liyah out of her shock. She'd had enough disapproval to last a lifetime. Her peace had been invaded. Her last night of solitude.

'I don't need rescuing.' A thought occurred to her and an acute sense of exposure made her ask, 'How long have you been there?'

'Long enough.' He sounded grim. 'You need to come out.'

Indignation filled her at his autocratic tone, reminding her of how little autonomy she had over her own life. 'I don't *need* to do anything, actually.'

'You're going to stay there all night? You'll freeze.'

It was true. The scorching desert temperatures fell precipitously at night. Liyah could already feel the chill of the water creeping into her bones.

'I can't come out. I don't have any clothes on.' Strangely, she didn't feel unsafe, even though this man was a complete stranger.

'I know.'

Liyah stopped treading water. 'You did spy on me.'

Yet, strangely again, the thought of him watching her strip and dive into the water wasn't making her feel indignant. It was making her feel... aware.

In the dusky half-light Liyah couldn't be entirely sure she wasn't dreaming. She could have sworn there had been no one else here when she'd arrived, but then, she hadn't exactly checked her surroundings thoroughly.

When she looked over the man's shoulder now, she could make out the shape of a tent amongst the trees on the far side of the oasis. And a horse. It whinnied softly and her horse answered.

'You're camping here?'

'For the night, yes.'

His voice was deep. Deep enough to reverberate in the pit of her belly. He had an accent she couldn't place. Mid-Atlantic, but with a hint of something else—something foreign. But also familiar to here. An intriguing mix. Yet she knew she'd never seen him before. He was a total stranger.

She should ask who he was, but for some reason the words wouldn't form on her tongue.

And he was right: she couldn't stay treading water all night.

'I need something to wear.' Her own clothes were scattered along the shoreline, but instead of going to pick them up the man reached behind his head and pulled off his robe.

Liyah's breath caught in her solar plexus when his bare chest was revealed. Massive and tightly muscled, with dark hair curling over his pectorals and a dark line dissecting his abdominals to disappear under the loosely fitting trousers that hung low on his lean hips.

'Here, take this.'

He held his robe outstretched to her from the shore. She swam towards the shallows until she could feel the ground beneath her feet. The water lapped around her shoulders.

She could see that the bottoms of his trousers were in the water. 'Your trousers are getting wet.'

'They'll dry.'

Again, Liyah wondered if she was in a dream. But no dream she'd ever had came close to this. She started to walk forward, feeling the resistance of the water against her body.

The waterline dropped lower, now just cov-

ering her breasts. Liyah stopped. She expected
the man to turn around, to show some respect.
But he didn't. *He'd already watched her.* Albeit
from behind.

Again, it didn't make her feel violated in any
way—it excited her.

If she was being rational for a second, *excited*
was the last thing she should be feeling. Scared.
Wary. Insulted. Indignant. Those were the things
she should be feeling. Yet she wasn't.

She should also be asking him to turn around.
But, again, the words wouldn't form in her mouth.
She was filled with a fire that made her feel rebellious and reckless. Surely just a reaction to everything that was happening to her—everything
that was expected of her? But she had a sense that
she was somehow regaining some control over a
life that had veered wildly out of control.

She also had an overwhelming compulsion to
go towards this complete stranger as she was.
Naked.

She took another step forward. The water
broke just over her breasts. Another step. Now her
breasts were bared to the man's dark gaze. She
could see him more clearly now. His eyes were
dark. His jaw defined. Tight. His gaze dropped.
Her nipples were already tight and hard from the
water. They tingled.

She kept moving forward and the water lapped
at her belly, then her hips, the tops of her legs and

thighs. Between her legs, where the centre of her body pulsed with heat.

In some corner of her brain she was aghast at herself for behaving with such wanton confidence. She wasn't this person who would allow a stranger to see her naked body. But here, in this place—this place that had been a sacred refuge to her for her whole life—she felt removed from reality. Removed from the confines of normal behaviour.

And this man was more than just a random stranger. She'd sensed it the minute she'd laid eyes on him. He held himself with the arrogance and confidence of a born leader. Entitled. Proud.

She stepped into the shallows and reached for the robe he held out. She pulled it on over her head, aware of that dark gaze watching as the fine material settled over her body, the bottom wet from the water.

The heat from his body lingered on the robe and made her skin prickle even more. Her breasts felt heavy. Tight.

'Thank you.' She sounded breathless.

'You're welcome.'

Strangely, even though she was covered again from neck to toe, she didn't feel any more protected from that penetrating gaze. Up close, she realised he was even more magnificent. A virile man in his prime. Tall. Broad. With dark olive skin that gleamed under the rising moon, stretched taut over hard muscles.

He held out a hand and Liyah looked at it for a long moment. The air was heavy around her. Heavy with a tension that had nothing to do with conflict or conversation. It was a tension that came from the crackling energy between them. A tension that came from this whole improbable situation.

In all her years of coming here she'd never met anyone else. Ever. But tonight, on the eve of her wedding to a man sight unseen, here was this compelling stranger. She wasn't usually prone to superstition, but it felt somehow…fated.

Tomorrow her life would change for ever, but tomorrow wasn't here yet… There was a whole night between now and then. A whole night of tantalising freedom left. The last piece of freedom she would have for some time.

Before she could think about it she put her hand into his. It was big. Slightly callused. Something about that evidence of hard work thrilled her. His fingers closed around hers and he tugged her out of the shallows and onto the sand.

Sharif had wondered if he was hallucinating. If he'd conjured up the goddess who had disappeared into the black depths of the oasis pool. But then she'd emerged, like Aphrodite, dark olive skin glistening like satin as the water sluiced over her body.

She was no marble statue, cold and rigid and pale. She was all woman. Flesh and bone. Limbs long and sleek.

And the hand in his now felt real enough.

Instinctively his thumb felt for her pulse and it throbbed at her wrist, echoing the throb in his blood.

'You are real...' he said, almost to himself.

Even though she was covered again, her naked image was imprinted on his brain. For ever, he suspected. He had watched her disrobe, too trans-fixed to say a word. Her body was carved from an erotic fantasy he hadn't even realised he'd had—strong and supple, athletic, but with curves that pronounced her a fertile woman in her prime.

Wide hips, small waist, long legs, lush bottom. And her breasts... Bigger than he would have guessed. Firm. Perfectly formed, with dark nipples that made his mouth water.

Dark tight curls at the juncture of her legs—he wanted to spread her there, see if she glistened...

'I am real.'

Her voice, husky, cut through the fever in Shar-if's head. His hand tightened around hers and he tugged her towards him. He caught her scent—roses and earth and sand and heat.

The other thing that slammed into his aware-ness now, up close, was the fact that she was stunningly beautiful—and tall. The top of her head would graze his jaw. Dark eyebrows framed huge almond-shaped eyes. He couldn't make out their colour in the light, but they weren't as dark as his. Straight nose. High cheekbones. That dark olive complexion.

His fingers itched to reach out and touch her, explore to see if her skin felt as satiny as it looked.

But her mouth…

His avid gaze stopped there. Her mouth was beyond provocative. A lush invitation to taste and explore. To crush under his as he enticed her to give up all her secrets.

Sharif felt dizzy. He had met and slept with some of the world's most beautiful women and not one had ever affected him like this. On a visceral, primal level. He knew that if he didn't have this woman—

He couldn't even finish that thought. *He would have her.* He had to.

Her thick, wild hair was wet, but he could see that it was already showing a tendency to curl again.

'Where did you come from?'

A man not remotely prone to superstitions or fantasies, Sharif felt for the first time in his life as if the world around him wasn't entirely…concrete.

'I could ask the same of you.'

The fact that she sounded equally at a loss to explain this set of events was little comfort.

'Does it matter?'

Sharif knew as soon as he asked it that it was a rhetorical question. They were here now. That was all that mattered.

She shook her head. 'No, it doesn't. Who we are doesn't matter either.'

Sharif barely heard the thread of desperation in her voice. It was only afterwards that he would recall it. Long afterwards.

But right now he felt a weight lift off his chest and shoulders. For the first time since he could remember he was with someone who had no idea who he was. There was no preconception, no misconception, no judgement, no expectation.

'Would you like something to eat?'

She blinked. 'Yes…okay. I'd like that.'

Keeping hold of her hand, Sharif led the woman over to his tent.

The tent that was set up in the shelter of the trees was larger than Liyah had expected, but the man still had to duck his head a little to go in. He had to be six foot five at least. Tall enough to make her feel small. And she was used to towering over most people.

Men in particular seemed to find her height a provocation. But not this one. The way he'd looked at her so intently just now… Her heart hadn't slowed down since she'd laid eyes on him.

Her eyes adjusted from the falling light out-side to the golden glow of lots of candles. There was a table set up with food, and a place-setting for one. There was a bed in the corner, large and luxurious, with jewel-covered throws.

Liyah looked away quickly, suddenly am-bushed by the memory of how it had felt to walk out of the water naked, with his dark gaze on her. She didn't want him to see her looking at the bed. He'd already crossed about a dozen boundaries that, if her rational brain was working, she would never have allowed anyone to cross. Not to men-tion a complete stranger.

He let her hand go and went over to the chair and pulled it out. 'Please…sit down.'

Liyah looked around. 'There's only one chair.'

'I'll find something. Please.'

It was so surreal that Liyah did as he bade, moving around the table to sit down. She felt him behind her, his hands close to her shoulders. Her hair was still damp. Heavy. It was too long, too unruly, but every time she got frustrated and de-termined to cut it she would think of the pictures she had of her mother, with the same long hair, and she'd lose the will to let it go.

Any memory or connection with her mother was so tenuous. And precious.

The man had disappeared behind a screen that

presumably hid the washing area. And now he reappeared, taking Liyah's breath away with his sheer physicality.

He had put on a plain white T-shirt and it made his dark olive skin look even darker. It highlighted the musculature of his chest, somehow making it more provocative than if he'd still been bare.

He put down a wooden stool on the opposite side of the table. For the first time she could look at him up close in the light and she was mesmerised.

He was breathtaking. His face was lean and sculpted, the low flickering candlelight casting shadows and making his skin gleam like burnished bronze. Hard jaw defined by stubble. Nose like a blade. Deep-set dark eyes. Fathomless.

His mouth was as strong as the rest of him, but wide. His lips were full, more than hinting at a sensual nature—as if Liyah hadn't noticed that as soon as she'd seen him. He oozed a sexual magnetism that had stunned her as effectively as if he'd shot her with a dart from a gun.

'Are you sure you don't want to take the chair? That doesn't look very comfortable.'

He shook his head and put an empty plate in front of her. 'Help yourself.'

At that moment Liyah realised she was famished. In the stress of the last week she'd barely eaten, and she didn't do well on low food supplies. The food looked…amazing. There was hummus and flatbread. Dolma vine leaves stuffed with meat. Succulent pieces of lamb with balls of spiced rice.

She picked a selection and put them on her plate. She heard a cork and saw him pour white wine into a glass.

He handed it to her. 'Drink?'

Liyah took it, and watched as he poured himself a glass. He raised it. The candles imbued the whole scene with a golden glow that didn't go anywhere near helping her to keep a grasp of reality.

'Here's to…unexpected encounters.'

Liyah lifted her glass. She could feel any desire to try to restore sanity, to remember who she was, where she was, fatally slipping away, to be replaced by a wholly different and far earthier desire.

She touched her glass to his and it made a low melodic chime. She echoed his words. 'To unexpected encounters.'

He lifted his glass to his mouth, and just before he took a sip he said, 'And what we make of them.'

CHAPTER TWO

'AND WHAT WE make of them.'

Liyah took a sip of her wine as she absorbed that comment. This man was altogether too bold and confident, but he'd woken something inside her. Something equally bold. If not as confident.

'Your eyes are green.'

Liyah looked at him. 'My mother's eyes were green.'

'Try the lamb. It's delicious.'

Liyah picked up a piece of lamb, along with some of the rice, and popped it into her mouth. The meat practically melted on her tongue and the spices in the rice made her taste buds come alive.

'You know this place well.'

It wasn't a question. Liyah swallowed her food and nodded. 'I've always come here. It's usually empty. It doesn't serve as a stopping point as it's so close to the city.' *To the palace.* She pushed her mind away from that reminder.

'Your bird is very tame. How old is he?'

Liyah bit back a smile. *'She.'*

The man smiled and she nearly fell off her chair. It changed him from being merely stupendously gorgeous to something not of this earth.

'I shouldn't have presumed.'

Liyah recovered her wits. 'She's been mine since I was a child. I trained her out here in the desert.'

'Does she have a name?'

Liyah felt self-conscious. No one had ever cared about her bird except for the falconer at the palace. 'Sheba.'

'Like the Queen? She is a beautiful bird.'

'Yes, she is.'

'Almost as beautiful as her owner.'

Liyah's mouth dried. Her heart thumped. He thought she was beautiful. But she knew that she wasn't really. She was too tall. Her hair was too wild. She couldn't fade gracefully into the background like other women. She always stuck out. Which made her think of her time in Europe. Her dark skin and height had marked her out from the start. Making her a target for people who wanted to exploit her for fun.

Others had told her she was beautiful back then too. And she'd lapped it up, starved of attention and in a new world where she'd felt out of place. But it had been a cruel lie.

This was a timely reminder. She had no idea who this man was and yet she was lapping up his attention like an eager puppy, having learnt nothing.

Liyah put down her napkin and went to stand, but the man caught her hand in his. He was frowning.

'Hey, where are you going?'

'I should leave. I don't know what I was thinking.'

Liyah pulled her hand free. The man stood up.

Just before she got to the opening to the tent, he said, 'Wait. Stop. Please.'

She didn't know him, but she sensed that he didn't say the word *please* much. It sounded rusty. Unused. She stopped and felt him come close behind her.

He said, 'Usually when I compliment a woman she doesn't run away.'

Liyah whirled around, incensed. 'I'm not running away. I've just realised that this is…' She stopped. She didn't even have words for what this was.

He supplied one. 'Crazy?'

'I didn't come here this evening expecting to find…you.'

'And yet here I am. I wasn't expecting company either. Far from it.'

Liyah looked up at him. He was too tall. So broad. He eclipsed everything around him.

'If I wanted to leave now, would you let me?'

He took a step back, looking almost affronted.

'Of course. You're free to go.' But then his expression changed and he said, '*If* you want to. But I don't think you do want to…'

He sounded so sure of himself. Part of Liyah wanted to prove him wrong. She wanted to turn, go outside, pick up her clothes and leave. But a much bigger part of her—the part that had felt little or no compunction about revealing her naked body to him—wanted to stay.

As if sensing her vacillation, he said, 'This thing between us…this connection…is not usual. You do know that?'

Of course she didn't. She'd believed that she'd wanted a man before—*correction, a boy*—but what she'd felt then had been nothing remotely like this swooping exhilarating rollercoaster of sensations. Even the food had tasted more delicious than anything she'd ever tasted before.

Fearing for her very sanity, she almost whispered, 'Are you actually real?'

He took a step towards her again and she could smell him, spicy and musky. He took her hand and lifted it up, placed it on his chest, over his heart.

She felt the strong rhythmic *thump-thump* under her palm. It sent a veritable tsunami of emotions through her. It was so illicitly intimate, yet reassuring at the same time.

Her father ran a conservative household. He didn't approve of displays of affection in public, or in private either. Any physical touch Liyah had experienced growing up had come at the brusque hands of nannies, or the women in the palace hammam.

She'd been in the hammam the day before, and to her eternal shame—because she didn't usually indulge in self-pity—a sense of loneliness and vulnerability had gripped her. She'd found tears running down her face. The only saving grace had been that she'd known they wouldn't be noticed during the ancient full-body-washing ritual.

Tears were a weakness that Liyah rarely indulged in. She had no reason to feel sorry for herself. She'd been born into a privileged world, albeit one that came with responsibilies and duties. She'd had a moment of believing she might escape them—when she'd been in Europe—but deep down she'd always known that her fate was not her own. She just hadn't known how that would manifest, or that it would manifest so dramatically.

And yet here she was, with her palm on this man's chest, his heart echoing the drumming of her blood. A sense of fatality gripped her. She had no idea what her husband-to-be was like, or who he was beyond a name—her own stubborn fault for not wanting to know…as if that might stop it happening—but tomorrow she would no longer be *this* anonymous woman.

No longer free to feel the heartbeat of a stranger under her palm. No longer free to swim naked or to take off on her horse when the whim took her. No longer—

'Kiss me, please,' she blurted out, the words rising up from an unstoppable place inside her.

Sharif's blood leapt. He wanted nothing more than to kiss this woman. And a lot more. But he forced himself to stop for a second.

He put his hand over hers on his chest. It felt incredibly feminine and delicate. 'Are you sure?'

He had seen the turmoil on her face just now, as if she was agonising. But now it was clear, determined.

She nodded. And said, 'Yes. I'm sure.'

Sharif took his hand from hers and put his hands on her upper arms, tugging her gently towards him until he could feel the heat of her body through the thin robe.

Her hair was already starting to curl wildly again. Her green eyes were huge. Unusual, and adding to her striking beauty. Not many had light-coloured eyes in this region. He wondered again for a second who she might be, but then pushed it aside. It didn't matter. All that mattered was this.

He pulled her closer until he could feel the lush curves of her body come into contact with his. *Dio*. He felt like a schoolboy with his first woman all over again. What the hell was *that* about?

She was looking up at him, both hands splayed

on his chest now. Lips parting, trembling slightly, her breath coming in little pants that made her breasts move against him.

He bent his head and covered her mouth with his, and even as a part of him was telling himself that this was no different from any other kiss he knew it was a lie.

Her lips were soft, but firm. Like her. All over. And he'd barely touched her but he was drowning. His hands tightened on her arms as if that would help anchor him as he deepened the kiss and tasted her sweetness.

She was hesitant at first, and that only heightened the eroticism of this relatively chaste kiss, but then she became bolder, matching his exploration with her own, nipping his tongue with her teeth. She wrapped her arms around his neck and came even closer…so close that he could feel the tantalising thrust of her hard nipples through the fabric of their clothes.

He pulled back, dizzy. He needed to see her, feel her. Now.

He must have spoken out loud because she took down her hands and arms and stepped back, dislodging his hold.

And as he watched she pulled his robe up and over her head, and dropped it to the floor of the tent.

He was looking at her as if he'd never seen a woman before. Which was ridiculous, because he had already seen her and she would be an idiot to think for a second that a man like this, who oozed sexuality and confidence, hadn't looked on lots of naked women.

Liyah's mouth felt swollen after that kiss. She could still taste him, dark and explicit, on her tongue.

But that black gaze devoured her now, lingering on her breasts, her belly, her waist. And down to the juncture between her legs. Her thighs.

'Turn around,' he ordered gruffly.

Liyah did so, welcoming momentary escape from that avid intensity. She heard movement behind her and then felt his heat before she felt him. *He was naked.*

He pulled her hair aside and over one shoulder. His hands came to her arms again and she felt his breath against her before his lips touched her bare skin.

'Okay?' he asked.

His consideration was not something she'd anticipated when she'd behaved so impetuously.

She nodded, and whispered, 'Yes. Please.'

Please keep going. Transport me from this world, from myself, for tonight, so I don't have to—

Liyah sucked in a gasp when the man's arms came under hers and he cupped her breasts in his big hands. His hair-roughened chest was at her back. And she could feel the potency of his hard body. Hard for her.

Heat grew at her core, making her wet. She groaned softly and fell back into him, her legs turning to jelly as one hand left her breast and travelled down, exploring her curves, over her belly to that place between her legs.

He drew her up against him, his erection cupped by her buttocks. With one hand, he explored her breast, fingers finding and trapping her nipple, his other hand gently encouraged her to part her legs, so that he could explore her there. Find the seam of flesh that was the last barrier to the evidence of how much she wanted him. Wanted this.

And then he was there, his fingers opening her up, sinking deep. She clutched at his arm, his hand. Pushing and pulling at the same time. Wanting him to keep doing what he was doing between her legs, but not wanting him to see how much she wanted it.

He whispered against her skin. 'It's okay... I know...'

She gave up fighting her response and opened up even more, allowing him to move his hand between her legs, his fingers seeking and finding and thrusting deep into her clasping flesh.

Liyah might have screamed—she wasn't even sure. All she knew was that he was turning her head so his mouth could fuse with hers as her whole body quivered and shook in his arms, the precursor to the storm he unleashed with a flick of his fingers.

Liyah was floating…and it was only when he laid her down on the bed that she realised she hadn't been floating at all. He'd just carried her over to the bed.

Her whole body was suffused with lingering ecstasy, the waves of orgasm making her inner muscles clench in reaction. She hadn't had an orgasm before…and now she understood.

A wave of gratitude swept through her, and before she could stop herself she said, 'Thank you.'

He came down on the bed beside her, long lean muscles rippling under all that dark skin. 'What for?'

Liyah clamped her mouth shut. She didn't want to admit she hadn't had an orgasm before, despite having had sex once. She didn't want to admit that she'd felt there must be something wrong with her because she hadn't enjoyed the experience, at all. It had been humiliating on so many levels and then afterwards—

She shut her mind to that.

She shook her head on the pillow. 'Nothing… Just, thank you.'

The man smiled.

Liyah bit her lip, wanting his mouth on hers again, drugging her, transporting her.

To mask her desire, she looked at him. She hadn't seen his naked body before…he'd been behind her. But now, as he lay alongside her, she let her gaze move down over the hard planes of his chest and his taut belly. To the dark hair between his legs and the rigid length of his erection. Veins ran up along the shaft, pulsing with blood. His thighs were thick and muscled.

Liyah felt dizzy, even though she was lying down. She glanced at him, feeling shy. He was watching her. She came up on one arm. 'Can I...? Touch you...?'

He lay on his back, his smile turning lazy. Knowing. 'Be my guest.'

Liyah came up on her knees. She tentatively put out a hand and placed it on his chest, feeling his heart beat again. It was thumping hard. Fast. She trailed it down over his belly. His muscles clenched. She looked at him quickly. He wasn't smiling any more.

He said, 'Go on.'

She was too intimidated by the silk and steel length of him to explore there just yet, so she traced her fingers over his thigh, marvelling at the sheer strength. His hips were narrow, where hers flared out. She'd never been so aware of a man and a woman's innate differences.

His body jerked at her touch, as if tempting her to touch him more intimately.

Her heart-rate leapt and after a moment of hesitation, she gave in to temptation, touching him experimentally.

He made a sound and she stopped.

He looked pained.

She asked, 'What is it?'

'Nothing, just…don't stop.'

Liyah curled her hand around him—as much as she could. There was a drop of moisture at the head and she had the inexplicable urge to lick it, taste his essence. She blushed at the thought.

'Let me see you.'

His voice sounded thick. Not sure what he meant, Liyah looked at him. He sat up slightly, muscles contracting. He took her arms and gently encouraged her to straddle him, placing her so she was spread across his thighs and facing him. Nowhere to hide. Exposed. Her skin prickled with excitement.

His hands moved down to her hips. He sat back against the plumped-up cushions. 'You have beautiful breasts.'

Liyah blushed again. She'd never thought much of her breasts. She'd always been a bit self-conscious of their size, wishing she had a more petite frame like her younger half-sisters. They felt heavy now.

He sat up and cupped them, looking at her briefly before bringing his hot mouth to first one and then the other, teasing her with open kisses and gentle nips on her skin, before placing his mouth where she was screaming internally to be touched.

He sucked one nipple and then the other, tugging at her flesh and making her head fall back at the sensation. He fed her flesh into his mouth as if savouring the most succulent food.

And then, with one hand, he touched her between her legs, where she was so exposed, and without warning she fell over the edge again, gasping in surprise and not a little terrified at this control he could wield so easily over her. It was as if he knew her body better than she did. A stranger.

When her world had stopped spinning she realised that he was lying back and her hands were digging into his chest. He pulled her down so that her breasts were crushed into his chest and then he moved her hair back, finding her mouth and kissing her.

Excitement built again when she felt his erection straining between them. Her body was moving instinctively against his, seeking friction. Seeking *more*.

He expertly manoeuvred her body so that she was sitting up again, poised over him. He held himself in his hand, the head nudging the entrance to her very core. She couldn't breathe. It was as if her body wept with the need to feel him inside her.

She let herself sink onto him slowly as he took his hand away and gripped her hip. He was big. She sucked in a breath but he lay still, letting her dictate the pace as she allowed her body to absorb all that heat and strength.

She held her breath as momentary discomfort made itself felt.

His hands tightened on her hips. 'Are you...?'

She focused on him, her vision blurred by all the sensations coursing through her body. What was he asking? If she was a—?

She shook her head. 'No, I'm not.'

But she'd only had sex once before, and she wasn't even sure if the experience counted, because it had felt nothing like this.

The discomfort had become something else—something much sharper and more pleasurable. Liyah started to move up and down slowly, letting her body get used to his.

They were both breathing heavily now, and Liyah felt sweat sheening her skin. Her movements became faster, and he held her hips lightly, but she could feel the need in him to hold her so that he could take control.

She felt infinitely powerful in that moment. But then her own frustration grew because she couldn't find the perfect rhythm that her body craved.

In a split second he'd manoeuvred them so that she was on her back and he looked down at her, his body still deeply embedded in hers.

He pulled out and her every muscle tensed,

waiting for the delicious slide of his body into hers again, but he stopped.

Hoping she didn't sound as desperate as she felt, Liyah said, 'Is something wrong?'

He pulled out fully and her body protested.

'Protection. I have no protection here.'

Liyah didn't understand for a second, and then she did. Relief flowed through her. 'It's okay. I'm on the pill.'

Sharif looked at the woman under him. Her wild hair was spread around her head. Her skin was flushed dark red, her eyes like bright green jewels. Lips plump.

The effort it had taken him to pull free from the clasp of her body made him shake. No woman—*ever*—had had this effect on him. Sex for him was usually a transitory physical satisfaction. Like scratching an itch. He'd always derived more pleasure out of the chase and the conquest than the actual *act*. He'd always been able to hold himself slightly aloof...

But here—now—that ability to remain aloof was incinerated. He'd almost forgotten his own rule. *Never sleep with a woman without protection*—because he had no intention of revisiting the sins of his father on an innocent child.

In another instant, with another woman, Sharif would have taken this as a wake-up call. His nat-

ural cynicism and distrust of people would have
flatlined his desire.

But his entire being ached with the need to
sheath himself inside her again and throw caution
to the wind, following the dictates of his body,
mind and soul to seek an oblivion he knew instinctively would eclipse anything he'd felt before.

He didn't even know her name.

He would never see her after this night.

Even more disturbing was this instinct that he
had to trust her. Or was that just needy desperation because he wanted her so badly?

'You're on the pill?'

She nodded. 'For over a year now. I wouldn't
lie about something like this. The consequences
for someone like me would be...unthinkable.'

Any sliver of sanity that might have pulled
Sharif back from the edge melted into a heat haze.
In this moment he believed her—and not just be-
cause he wanted to.

He said, 'I'm clean. I got checked recently.'

*Even though he never made love without pro-
tection.*

Her hands went to his chest, palms flat. 'I trust
you.'

I trust you.

No women—*no person*—had ever said that to
him before. He had never been in the business of
fostering enough intimacy to invite statements
like that. *Until now.*

But he didn't want to dwell on that. Not when every muscle in his body was screaming with the need to join his body with this woman's.

He forced himself to say, 'Are you sure?'

She nodded. 'Please—I want this. I want you.'

He found the slick folds that parted, oh, so easily when he pushed against her, and couldn't help the low groan of intense satisfaction when he sheathed himself inside her silky tight embrace again. The fact that this didn't just feel like *sex* was also something he didn't want to dwell on.

He forced himself to control his thrusts, letting her get used to his body. He knew he was big, and he could tell she was inexperienced—even if she wasn't a virgin.

Gradually he felt her body adjust to his, saw the way her cheeks flushed a darker pink. The way she bit her lip. The way she moved under him, lifting her hips. Her hands explored him, and if she wasn't careful she was going to push him off the edge way before he was ready.

He caught her hands and raised them above her head, linking their fingers. He said, 'Spread your legs wider for me.'

She did, and he sank even deeper. She let out a low moan. Sharif let her go and slid his hand under her back, arching her up so that he could find and suck one hard nipple into his mouth, rolling the taut peak before nipping gently.

Her movements became more frenzied, and

he felt the telltale flutters along his length as he drove deep and hard. Sweat sheened their skin as they raced to the pinnacle, and it took more control than Sharif had ever had to call on in his life to ensure that she reached it before he did.

She arched up, her whole body taut like a bow, as her orgasm held her high before ripping through her body all the way to her inner muscles, which clenched so hard around Sharif that he was no longer capable of holding back the flood of ecstasy that wiped his brain clean of every single coherent thought.

Today

Liyah woke with a start. She was lying in an unfamiliar bed in unfamiliar surroundings and her body felt…

A rush of heat flashed through her mind when she recalled where she was.

And with whom.

The nameless man.

He was lying on his front beside her, but not touching her. One arm was carelessly hanging over the edge of the bed, the other was bent up over his head. His face was turned to the side, towards her.

Even in sleep he looked fierce. Strong. The stubble lining his jaw was darker…

Her wide awake gaze—tracked down over

the sleek muscles, no less impressive at rest. Those narrow hips. His buttocks—firm. A pulse throbbed between her legs when she thought of the sheer power of his body thrusting into hers, so deep she'd seen stars.

A wave of emotion took her by surprise. After her first dismal sexual experience in Europe she'd suspected that there might be something wrong with her. But after last night…

This man had restored a very wounded part of her soul. And her confidence. He'd looked at her as if he'd never seen a woman before. He'd touched her as reverently as if she was infinitely precious, and then he'd made love to her as if he had been starving for something only she could give him.

She'd fallen into a pleasure-induced coma after that first time and had woken in his arms to find him carrying her over to a steaming hot bath that had been hidden behind the screen.

She hadn't even been aware of how tender her muscles were until she'd felt the hot water soothe them. Still stunned after what had happened, she'd been incapable of speech. He'd climbed into the bath behind her, spreading his legs down alongside hers, and had tucked her hair up in a knot before soaping her all over, his big hands making her feel delicate and precious for the first time…*ever*.

She'd turned her head, afraid of the clutch of

emotion in her chest—afraid of what it meant and that he'd see it —and had found his mouth. Firm and hot. She'd turned in the bath until she was straddling him, the silky water making it easy to glide over him and sink down onto his erection. The movement of their bodies, as if they'd been made for each other, had quickened as the fever of lust had taken them over, the water splashing all around the tub going unnoticed in their race to find nirvana again.

She had only the vaguest memory of him lifting her out of the bath, rubbing her down briskly with a towel and laying her back down on the bed, of his steely warmth surrounding her, his hand on her breast...

Yet here she was now. Her bones felt liquid.

She noticed, almost lazily, that there were pink trails in the sky outside, just visible above the opening in the tent.

Pink trails heralding dawn.

The dawn of her wedding day.

Suddenly Liyah wasn't feeling lazy any more. Panic gripped her belly. She was due to have henna painted on her hands and feet this morning, in preparation for the afternoon's ceremony.

She had to go. *Now.*

She managed to leave the sumptuous bed without waking him, and stole to the opening of the tent. But there she stopped, giving in to temptation and taking one last look, knowing she'd never see him again. Knowing that she might always wonder if she'd dreamt this night up.

Her eyes devoured his majestic form. Even though he was sprawled in louche splendour across the bed, he was no less impressive or intimidating. His body and his face would be imprinted on her memory. For ever.

That clutch of emotion caught at Liyah again. What had happened here had been so...unexpected. Unprecedented. And magical. It would be her secret to carry with her, deep inside, where no one would ever find it.

Least of all her new husband.

When Sharif woke his head felt fuzzy, as if he'd had too much to drink. And his body felt pleasantly achy. Heavy. But also light.

But he hadn't had too much to drink.

He'd just had the most intensely erotic experience of his life.

Sharif jacknifed up to sit in the bed as vivid memories assailed him.

But beside him was an empty space. No sign of the wild-haired temptress with the green eyes who had rendered him insensible with desire.

Desire? He grimaced at that. Desire was too ineffectual a word for what he'd felt for her from the moment he'd seen her revealed by the pool.

A wave of lust gripped him as the previous night came back in glorious Technicolor. The way she'd sat astride him, taking him deep into her body, the look of awe on her face, her cheeks darkened with pleasure. And how it had felt when her secret inner muscles had milked him—

Dio. Sharif never dwelled on sex with lovers. He had it—he moved on.

He got out of the bed, feeling dizzy for a moment. Dizzy after a night of unbridled pleasure. He sensed the tent was empty and walked to the entrance, pulling back the material over the opening.

Dawn was bathing the oasis in deep pinks and golds. Sharif stepped out. Naked. The cool air made his skin prickle, but so did the fact that there was no sign of the woman.

Her horse was gone.

She was gone.

He walked over to the pool. Its serene surface left no hint of the unearthly goddess who had disappeared into its depths only to emerge and prove that she'd been all too earthly.

Sharif's skin prickled even more, and it had nothing to do with the cool air and everything to do with a sense of exposure. Had she in fact existed at all? Or had it been a particularly lurid dream? Was he so jaded that he'd conjured up an erotic fantasy to entertain himself on the eve of his wedding to a woman sight unseen?

In fact the more he thought about it, the more he found it almost easier to believe it hadn't happened. He was no saint, but neither was he inclined to 'instalust' or casual sex with a stranger. Usually his women were carefully vetted.

Not that it stopped them from crying to the tabloids when he ended their liaisons, a snide inner voice reminded him.

He ignored the voice. And then went cold as he thought of something else. They hadn't used protection. He'd taken her at her word when she'd mentioned being on the pill.

He shook his head. It couldn't have happened. He *never* indulged in unprotected sex. A man like him was a magnet for women who wanted to secure their lives by having his baby. And he was not in the market for babies. Not now. Not ever.

In a bid to wake himself out of this reverie and come back to sanity, Sharif stepped into the water and dived deep into its inky depths. The shock of the water made his brain freeze, and only when his lungs were ready to burst did he come back up to the surface.

As he sucked in deep breaths his mind cleared. It *had* been a dream. Lurid and very real, yes, but a dream. That was the only way he could explain it. And he always had crazy dreams when he was in the desert. Admittedly, never like that...

Sharif walked out of the water, a sense of almost relief coursing through him. Relief that it hadn't been real, but also a tinge of regret. But of course she hadn't been real—a woman like that couldn't possibly be...

Just then something caught his peripheral vision. Something white. He went over to it. It was near the shoreline, on the ground.

Sharif stooped down and picked it up. A scrap of material. White. Cotton. Plain. Underwear.

A flash of memory came back to him—the woman stepping out of her clothes. Diving into the water.

She *had* been real.

The relief that coursed through him made a mockery of his assurance that it had all been a dream, but Sharif's mouth firmed. It might have been real, and he might have acted completely out of character, but she was gone now, like a ghost, and she would have to remain that way. Within a few hours he was to marry a woman he'd never met. He didn't need the distraction of an erotic temptress.

It was time to avenge his mother's betrayal and her death, and nothing would get in his way.

CHAPTER THREE

'YOUR WIFE MAY now reveal her face.'

Liyah's heart was thumping so hard she was surprised no one else could hear it. It had taken off like a racehorse, obliterating the escalating dread, the minute she'd seen her husband-to-be and recognised him as her nameless lover from the previous night.

No longer nameless.

He was Sheikh Sharif Bin Noor Al Nazar. Or, as he was better known in America and Europe, Sharif Marchetti, CEO of a vast luxury conglomerate.

This information had been supplied to her by the gossiping women at the henna painting ceremony earlier that day, while there had also been mention of how handsome he was.

Liyah's head had been too full of the previous night to take much notice.

He was resplendent in Al-Murja royal dress, which made him look even taller and broader. The cream silk of his royal robes, with gold thread piping, enhanced his dark skin tone. He wore no headdress. But Liyah noticed that his hair had been trimmed since last night. And his jaw was clean-shaven.

She remembered the graze of his stubble against her inner thighs...

She slammed a door on that incendiary memory.

The shock that had hit her like a body-blow as soon as she'd recognised him still gripped her, keeping her in a sort of paralysis. The only thing that had given her the time to absorb that shock was the fact that he hadn't yet recognised *her*. But he was about to...

The women came forward—her sister Samara was one of her attendants today—and they deftly and far too quickly removed the elaborate face shield that was a traditional part of weddings in Taraq, and had been for hundreds of years.

Liyah blinked as her eyes adjusted to the brightness of the throne room in the royal palace. A grand description for what was really a modest fortress.

She looked up at her husband with dread lining her belly and saw the expressions chase across his face as if in slow motion. Recognition. Confusion. And then shock, disbelief. Anger.

And then his mouth opened and he uttered one word. *'You!'*

Somehow—miraculously—no one seemed

to have caught Sharif's exclamation of recognition, and the ceremony finished as Liyah's hand was placed over his—the moment when she was deemed to be his wife.

Her hand was covered in the dark, intricate stains of henna. The red swirls swam a little in front of her eyes and she had to suck in a breath, terrified she might faint. The heavy robes and headdress she wore weren't helping.

Her gaze had slid away from his as soon as he'd spoken, but she could feel those dark eyes on her, boring into her, silently commanding her to look at him.

She felt numb, and she welcomed it, because if the numbness wore off then she knew she would be subjected to an onslaught of sensations and memories.

When she'd returned to the palace earlier, and undergone the pre-wedding bathing ritual, she'd lamented her mystery lover's touch and smell being washed from her body, even though she knew how inappropriate it would have been to go to another man while his imprint was still on her.

But he was no longer a mystery. He was her husband. And that fact filled her with so many conflicting feelings that she felt dizzy all over again.

They were led in a procession with the guests and both families into another formal room. The ballroom. Where a lavish feast had been laid out.

Normally weddings in Taraq would be three and four-day affairs—but, as her father had told her, this was to be a much briefer celebration.

Liyah and Sharif were seated at the top table, side by side. She took her hand from his and sat down, studiously avoiding looking to her right, where he sat. The ring that had been placed on her finger during the ceremony felt heavy. She'd barely looked at it—a thick, ornate gold ring, with a bluish stone in a circular setting surrounded by diamonds.

The King of Al-Murja, a man as tall and dark and handsome as Sharif, sat nearby, looking austere. As austere as her husband.

Husband. She felt dizzy again, even though she was sitting down.

Liyah cursed herself now for not having looked him up. If she had, she would have known who he was at the oasis.

And would that have changed her behaviour?

Liyah couldn't say how she would have reacted last night even if she'd known who he was. It was all too much to process.

And then, from her right, came a low and steely tone. 'Look at me, *wife.*'

Liyah gulped and slowly turned her head to meet those far too memorable dark eyes. She noticed now that there were gold rings around his irises. So not totally dark. Golden. Molten.

'So what was that last night? Were you trying out the wares before you committed to marriage with a stranger? Should I be flattered you deemed me suitable?'

His voice was cold enough to make her shiver—a big difference from how he'd sounded last night. The mid-Atlantic twang mocked her now. As did her instinct last night that he was not just *anyone*.

'No,' she croaked. 'It wasn't like that. I had no idea who you were.'

He made a rude sound. 'I find that hard to believe.'

His accusing tone broke Liyah out of her shocked paralysis. 'Wait… Did you know who I was?'

'No.'

A dart of hurt lanced her. He'd been equally disinclined to know about her. But she shouldn't be surprised—after all her sister had told her. *He just wants a wife. He doesn't care who that is.*

'Then I could accuse you of the same—maybe you did know who I was and you wanted to make sure *I* was suitable.'

'You weren't a virgin. That would make you very unsuitable to some.'

Liyah flushed at that. In this part of the world he would be within his rights to reject her on those grounds… Except the time to do it would have been the moment he'd recognised her.

'Are you going to say something?' Liyah immediately thought of the potential repercussions for her younger sister, who might be denied the husband she wanted to punish Liyah.

But Sharif shook his head slowly. 'No. I'm not a hypocrite. I'm far from a virgin. I don't expect my wife to be. Anyway, that's not what this marriage will be about.'

Liyah looked at him. She frowned. 'What's that supposed—?'

But she was cut off when the music started, drowning out what she'd been about to say. She had to face forward to watch the traditional dancers.

Her brain was racing, wanting to know what Sharif had meant. She cursed herself again for not having looked him up. She would have been better prepared. But it was too late to dwell on regrets. Or on reckless decisions made in the heat of the moment.

She'd never expected to see him again but now he was her husband. And she would have to deal with the consequences.

Sharif's blood was boiling as he sat beside his brand-new wife. Aaliyah. She now had a name. The woman who had driven him senseless with lust only a few hours ago. The same woman he'd suspected of being a figment of his imagination.

He didn't believe for a second that she hadn't known who he was last night. It was too conveniently serendipitous that she'd just happened to visit the oasis when he'd been there.

Someone must have told her that he hadn't arrived at the palace with his entourage. And she'd come to investigate her future husband. The thought that she'd been laughing at him the whole way through the marriage ceremony, behind her veil, set his nerves on edge.

Little happened in Sharif's life that he wasn't in control of. And this was not how he'd envisaged his marriage starting—with his blood boiling over with shock, anger and, even worse, *lust*.

Even though her body was now covered in the voluminous red and white traditional wedding robes of Taraq, Sharif could picture every dip and hollow. How she'd looked when she'd stepped out of the water in front of him, water sluicing down over endless curves and gleaming skin. The long sleek limbs. Her breasts, perfectly shaped and heavy...the juncture between her legs where dark hair curled enticingly, inviting him to explore—

Dio. He'd planned on making the most of his wife in the coming weeks, having her by his side at as many events as possible to ensure that the Marchetti Group brand was at its most stable and valuable for when he put his plans into motion.

By his side. Not in his bed. And most definitely *not* under his skin.

The last woman in the world he'd ever expected to see again, who he wanted nowhere near him,

was in fact now his wife. And as his wife, she
would be in close proximity at all times. Whether
he liked it or not.

'Liyah…you look so sophisticated. I've never seen
you like this.'

Liyah grimaced at her reflection in the mirror. The shift dress and matching jacket were in
pastel pink. She hated pink. She hated anything
too girly and always had, preferring a far more
relaxed and casual tomboy aesthetic.

She'd barely even taken notice of the women
who had measured her up the day after her father had allowed her to take Samara's place as
Sharif's bride. She'd been too impatient to see
her horse, whom she hadn't seen in months, while
she'd been in Europe.

But now she knew why she'd been measured
up.

Because her…her *husband* had provided this
going-away outfit. And another bag containing
a change of clothes, sleepwear, underwear and
toiletries.

She thought she looked ridiculous. Her hair
was too wild and unruly for an outfit like this, but
it was too late to try and tame it. And, even worse,
suddenly she felt nervous. She'd managed to avoid
Sharif while the reception had been underway
and they'd been surrounded by a hundred people,

but now she would be stepping onto a plane with him and there would be nowhere to hide.

'My hair…my hair is too much.'

Samara stepped up behind her and pulled her hair back into a low ponytail. 'Your hair is beautiful, Liyah, like the rest of you.'

Samara rested her chin on Liyah's shoulder and she met her sister's dark gaze in the mirror. Liyah didn't even share the same eye colour as her siblings. She really was the cuckoo in the nest.

Samara's pretty face was serious. 'Thank you, Liyah, for what you've done. You have no idea how much—'

A rising swell of emotion made Liyah turn around. She clasped her sister close before the emotion became too much to push down. 'I know,' she whispered. 'I know. Just be happy, Sammy, okay? Marry Javid and be happy.'

At that moment Liyah truly wished for her sister that she wouldn't be disappointed by love. Or destroyed by it, like their father.

Her sister nodded against her. She pulled back, dark eyes bright with tears. But she forced a smile. 'I'll miss you.'

'And I'll miss you. But call me any time, okay?'

Samara nodded again.

Maids entered to take Liyah's bags down to where her husband waited in the royal courtyard and Liyah followed them. Samara was the only one who had come to say goodbye. Liyah hated it that it still hurt. That some small vulnerable part of her had still hoped that she'd be important to her family. To her father.

She stopped in the shadows just under the massive stone archway that led outside. Sharif was pacing back and forth. He saw the maids coming out with the bags and flicked his wrist to look at his watch, clearly impatient. But Liyah couldn't move.

Gone were the elaborate gold and cream robes of the regal Sheikh—and gone was the wild nameless man who had seduced her into a place of heated insanity last night. In their place was another incarnation…this one even more intimidating.

His tall, lean body was sheathed in an immaculate three-piece dark suit. A white shirt, open at the neck, highlighted his dark skin. He *should* have looked more civilised. More urbane. But if anything he looked even more elemental. Wild. Dangerous.

Even though she'd slept with him, she felt in that moment that she'd never truly know him, and a little shiver skated over her skin. A kind of premonition that as soon as she stepped out of this shadow and into the sunlight, under his gaze and his protection, her life would never be the same. And she knew it wouldn't—for obvious reasons, and also for much deeper and more secret reasons that she really did not want to investigate right now.

The self-protective walls she'd cultivated her whole life suddenly felt very flimsy.

The sun was setting, bathing everything with a golden glow. It had been around this time yesterday that Liyah had left the palace to ride out to the oasis.

Suddenly, in spite of everything, she had a sense that she didn't regret what had happened at the oasis. It had been too earth-shattering to regret. It had changed something inside her.

A man who looked like an aide hurried over to Sharif's side, and Liyah heard Sharif speak in a low, harsh tone.

'Find her.'

Steeling herself, Liyah stepped forward out of the shadows. 'I'm here. Ready to go.'

Sharif turned around, his whole body reacting with a jolt of awareness just to hearing her husky voice.

Damn.

She had changed out of the traditional wedding robes that dated back to when her family had been Bedouin nomads. Sharif had asked an assistant to ensure she received appropriate clothes for her transition into his world as his wife, but clearly he hadn't researched much about her, or what she looked like.

Nor did you, reminded an inner voice.

He quashed the sting of his conscience when he thought of how little it had registered when he'd been asked if he would mind marrying the eldest Princess of Taraq and not her sister.

He'd agreed, and in the same instant moved on to the next item on his agenda—because it really didn't matter to whom he was married. All he needed was a wife.

But now he was aware of the significance of having chosen another woman, however carelessly.

Would the other sister have been sent to the oasis to seduce him, too?

The pastel pink did nothing for her skin tone, and the plain design of the dress effectively hid the spectacular curves that he couldn't stop seeing in his mind's eye. All he could think about was the fact that this woman needed to be dressed in bold and vibrant colours. With jewels at her throat and ears. Her wrists. Arms. And with silk and satin clinging to every luscious inch of her body.

Nothing could really detract from her sheer luminous beauty, though. Not even her unstyled pulled-back hair, or the fact that her face was scrubbed clean. Sharif couldn't recall the last time a woman had made so little effort for him.

Irritation at his reaction to her and this whole situation, which had morphed beyond what he'd expected, made his voice sharp. 'We should leave. My plane is waiting at the airfield.'

He noticed how she lifted her chin at his tone and something flashed in those stunning green eyes. A flash of defiance. His blood sizzled and he gritted his jaw.

He ignored his driver standing to attention and opened the back door of the Jeep himself. 'Please.'

He'd said *please* more than he'd ever said it in his life within the past twenty-four hours.

Aaliyah moved forward, the nude high heels making her legs look even longer and more lissom, reminding him of how strong her thighs were. Firm and lean from riding her thoroughbred stallion to deserted oases so she could swim naked and tempt men. Tempt *him*.

Suddenly the thought that he might not have been the only one to see her like that made his blood spike to dangerous levels.

He gritted his jaw even harder as her clean, unmanufactured scent tickled his nostrils as she got into the car and her dress slid up, revealing a taut and silky-smooth thigh. He'd noticed that the heels put her tantalisingly closer to his mouth too.

He closed the door and walked around the vehicle to get into the front beside the driver. The sooner they were back in his world, on his turf, where he could regain some sense of control, the better.

* * *

Liyah woke with a start, not sure were she was. There was a voice.

'Mrs Marchetti?'

Who was Mrs Marchetti?

It came again, insistent, along with a peremptory knock on wood.

She was on her husband's private jet.

It all came rushing back.

'Mrs Marchetti? We're landing in half an hour.'

Liyah sat up in the bed. The voice was on the other side of the bedroom door. 'Thank you. I'm awake,' she croaked out.

'Would you like some breakfast?'

Liyah saw the pink trails across the sky outside. They'd chased the dawn from the Middle East to the west.

'Just some coffee would be lovely, thank you.'

She was about to land in a whole new world and life. She'd expected this to be happening with a stranger. Well, he still was a stranger. But one she knew intimately.

Liyah saw the en suite bathroom and went in, groaning when she saw the frizz ball her hair had become. Her face was creased too, from where she'd lain down. She felt sticky.

She noticed that someone had left her bags in the bedroom and took the opportunity to freshen up, pulling out a pair of dark trousers and a long-sleeved cashmere top. Simple, elegant. Better than the powder-pink dress.

She took a quick shower, tying her hair up out of the way. It was too much of a job to get into washing and drying it now.

When she'd dried off and changed, she found a mercifully flat pair of shoes and took a breath and went into the cabin.

She could see Sharif's dark head over his seat-back. When she came closer he was engrossed in his laptop. He glanced at her as she came along-side him and slid into the seat on the other side of the aisle. She only realised then that she'd left her hair in a knot on the top of her head, too wild to let loose.

The steward came over with a steaming coffee and Liyah smiled her thanks, accepting it grate-fully, hoping she didn't look too dishevelled.

She took a sip, relishing the hot tart taste, and then risked another look at Sharif. He closed his laptop and she noticed stubble on his jaw. He'd taken off his jacket but still wore the waistcoat of the suit. Shirtsleeves rolled up. He was utterly civilised and *un*civilised all at the same time. A potent mix.

'Did you work all night?'

He accepted a coffee from the steward too. He looked at her, arching a brow. 'Concerned about me, Aaliyah?'

His voice made her insides tighten with awareness. This man was so dangerous. And he already knew so much about her. Too much.

Up until the cataclysmic moment when she'd realised who her husband was, she'd felt safe in the knowledge that her uncharacteristic behaviour would never be scrutinised in the cold light of day. But the universe was laughing at her now. Not only would her behaviour be scrutinised, but she'd married a man whose only impression of her was based on the illicit night they'd shared together. And she had no defence. She'd been bolder and more brazen than at any other time in her life.

'Don't call me Aaliyah. It's Liyah. Please.'

'Liyah, then.' His gaze dropped, taking in her change of clothes. 'Dark matte colours and pinks do nothing for you,' he observed. 'We'll remedy that. I have lots of events lined up that you'll be required to attend by my side.'

Liyah flushed at the way he assessed her so coolly, as if she was some kind of mannequin. Feeling defensive she said, 'I didn't choose the clothes. They were picked for me.'

'Well, you didn't offer any information on what you preferred,' Sharif pointed out.

Liyah said nothing, because she had scant interest in fashion or trends, and she wasn't sure she would have been adept at knowing what *did* suit her. The fact that she suspected this man did made her feel defensive all over again. She really knew next to nothing about him.

'My father said you control a…a luxury conglomerate?'

His dark gaze narrowed on her face. She felt very bare. Not that she was used to wearing make-up, but she'd like some kind of armour right now.

'Yes, I run it with my two half-brothers.'

So, he had family. Liyah absorbed that.

Sharif frowned. 'You really didn't know who I was at the oasis?'

She shook her head. 'I figured there would be plenty of time to learn about who you were. After all, we're married now, for better or worse. For a long time.'

'You weren't much interested in the prenuptial agreement. My staff told me you only glanced through it before signing.'

Liyah shrugged. 'I thought that would please you?'

'It intrigues me. I don't know a woman who wouldn't have gone through the document with a team of lawyers and dissected it to within an inch of its life before engaging in negotiatons for the maximum they could get their hands on.'

'The women you know don't sound very nice.'

A muscle in his jaw ticked. 'That could very well be the case, but as one of the wealthiest people on the planet I do tend to attract a certain type. So what makes you different? I know you don't have your father's fortune to fall back on, because your family is all but bankrupt—like your country. Hence the eagerness to marry you, or anyone, off.'

Liyah blinked. 'So it's true…the rumour about the fiscal debt in Taraq?'

Sharif nodded. 'Your father and his ministers have overextended themselves hugely in redeveloping the country.'

Liyah had heard the rumours—especially when she'd been abroad—but hadn't known if they were true or not. Naturally her father would never share such information with her. Not even when she was helping dig her own country out of debt with this marriage.

'I don't depend on my father for an income or an inheritance,' Liyah said. 'He wrote me out of the family will long ago.'

'Why?'

'Because my mother left an inheritance to me, her only child. My father couldn't touch it, and I inherited when I was eighteen. It's probably nothing compared to the wealth you command, but it's enough to keep me secure.'

'That's the only thing you checked in the prenup—to make sure that our marriage didn't give me any rights over the money you have independently.'

Liyah nodded. 'So I don't need anything from you.'

An expression crossed his face, too fast to decipher, but Liyah thought it was scepticism.

He said, 'That's refreshing to know. But let me know how you feel when I initiate our divorce and you've become used to a life of comfort and luxury beyond your wildest dreams.'

'Divorce?' They'd only just got married.

'You really should have read that prenuptial agreement properly. It's all in there. When you signed the contract, the day before the wedding— hours before we met at the oasis—you agreed to a divorce at the earliest in six months and at the latest in a year's time. This is a marriage in name only—purely for appearances.'

Liyah let this sink in. She should be feeling relief right now, at the thought that not only was this a marriage in name only but that it was also to be shortlived. But what she was feeling was more ambiguous. Curiosity...

'Why such a specific timeframe?'

'Because I only need a wife until such time as I don't need one any more. Once certain...objectives have been met.'

The air steward approached them again, to inform them that they'd be landing any minute and to ask them to make sure they were buckled in.

Liyah's head was buzzing with this information. If what Sharif was saying was true, then within a year at the most she'd have her freedom again. And by that time Samara would be married into her new family, so Liyah wouldn't have any reason to return to a place that had never really welcomed her. She really would be free.

So why didn't that induce joy?

The wedding ring on Liyah's finger felt very heavy all of a sudden, and she twisted it absently on her finger.

Sharif asked sharply, 'Does it not fit?'

Liyah looked at him. She shook her head. 'It fits fine…it's just…*big.*'

The plane touched down smoothly at that moment. As the roar of the throttle eased, and the plane made its way to the hangar where they would disembark, Liyah asked, 'This really was always intended to be a marriage in name only?'

Sharif nodded. 'As per the prenuptial agreement—it's all there in black and white.'

'But what…?' Liyah stopped, suddenly hesitant.'

Sharif lifted a brow. 'What…?'

Liyah could feel herself getting hot again. 'What about the fact that we…?' She stopped again, unable to articulate the words.

'Slept together?'

She nodded.

Sharif's expression hardened. 'That was a mistake. It won't happen again. This marriage isn't about that.'

Liyah couldn't look away from Sharif's hard expression. *'It won't happen again.'* A word trembled on her tongue. *Why?* But she stopped herself from letting it slip out, cursing herself for not realising sooner.

She'd been inexperienced. He hadn't. Clearly what had been a transformative experience for her had not been nearly as earth-shattering for him, and she felt mortified now for assuming otherwise.

She should be welcoming this development. The fact that he didn't really want a wife. He'd seduced her so easily. She'd lain down and bared her entire body and soul to him. She'd behaved totally out of character. Did she really want to risk revealing herself to him again? *No.*

The plane had come to a stop now, and staff were opening doors. Liyah gathered her things and avoided Sharif's eye, terrified that he might read something she couldn't hide.

Disappointment.

CHAPTER FOUR

ABOUT AN HOUR after they'd landed at the airfield Sharif watched Liyah walk around the vast space of his penthouse. A helicopter had brought them from the airfield to the building Sharif owned, where he had an apartment at the very top.

Liyah had looked mesmerised as they'd flown over the iconic city.

'Have you been to New York before?' he'd asked her.

She'd just shaken her head, eyes wide and glued to the canopy of tall sparkling buildings below. It had made Sharif look down too, for the first time in a long time. Normally he was in such a hurry to get to the next place, next meeting...

Now she walked through the vast open living space, and Sharif noted it dispassionately through her eyes. Impeccably decorated, with a neutral background of varying shades of grey. The furniture was sleek and elegant—antique. Works of art, on the walls and dotted around the room on tables, provided pops of colour and texture.

It struck him now that he'd never really felt fully connected with this space. He had no more attachment to this apartment than he did to any hotel suite.

Massive curtains were pulled back from floor-to-ceiling windows and a huge set of French doors that led out to a terrace overlooking Central Park. Liyah stood at the window and looked out.

Her hair was still up in a messy knot. The trousers and top she'd changed into did little to hide her body. She could be a model, with her height and proportions. But, her generous curves would put her in the plus size bracket —which was ridiculous, Sharif knew, because she was a perfectly healthy weight.

It was an aspect of the fashion industry that was slowly changing to reflect a far more accurate depiction of women's bodies, and not before time.

He didn't welcome the hum of electricity that seemed to have become a permanent fixture in his blood since she'd been revealed at the wedding. *Since last night.* He defended himself. She was truly stunning, even as pared back as she was right now. And he was only human. He'd always appreciated a beautiful woman.

But something prickled over Sharif's skin as he contemplated what a knockout she would be when she was dressed to impress. He had a feeling that she would easily transcend the most beautiful women he'd ever seen. And he inhabited a world where beauty wasn't just a given. It was expected. Demanded.

He resolved to speak to his team about making sure there were no skeletons in her closet that might derail his plans. But he was sure there weren't. The Mansour royal family weren't renowned for creating headlines—which was one of the reasons he'd decided to make the most of the diplomatic marriage.

Liyah was still trying to get her bearings after the helicopter ride that had whisked them over to the island of Manhattan, to this tall, gleaming spire of steel where they'd landed on the roof. She looked over the expanse of Central Park nearby—less lush than usual at this time of year, in late winter, but still beautiful.

A tiny bubble of hysteria rose inside her as she realised that it was no wonder she couldn't get her bearings. Her feet had literally hardly touched the ground since they'd landed. And was this how her new husband lived? In the clouds? Far above the mere mortals below? He probably got whatever was the opposite of a head rush if he had to go down to ground level.

She could feel him behind her, albeit a few feet away. Looking at her. Was he trying to figure her out? Or was she so inconsequential to him that she wasn't even worth that?

She turned around and felt an immediate rush of awareness when she found that he *was* looking at her. Hands in pockets. Supremely at home against this luxurious backdrop. She might be from a royal family but she knew that whatever riches and privileges she'd grown up with could never have prepared her for *this* world. They were at another level now. Literally. He could probably buy and sell her entire country a few times over and still have change.

Liyah folded her arms, feeling self-conscious. 'If you don't mind me saying, you look as if you were doing just fine without a wife.'

Sharif moved then, with a fluid athletic grace that made Liyah's mouth go dry. He took off his jacket and draped it gracefully over a chair and then sat down on a couch, his large body all at once relaxed and yet alert. Primed. He had a stillness about him that was seriously unnerving, but also mesmerising. Like a predator that looked benign until it struck with deadly precision.

He put out a hand, 'Please, sit—make yourself at home.'

Liyah's mouth compressed as she took in the vast array of sumptuous couches and chairs covered in smooth soft velvet. Tactile and yet intimidating. Because they looked as if they'd never been touched. She chose an armchair at a right angle to his couch and sat gingerly.

Sharif said, 'I can assure you that I do indeed

need a wife at this particular juncture. But tell me something…why did you offer yourself up in your sister's place?'

The thought that he could be here right now with Samara and not *her* sent a dark shard of something very disturbing deep into Liyah's gut. *Jealousy?*

Liyah felt prickly after that disturbing revelation. 'Samara is only nineteen.'

'Which, as you know, in Taraq and Al-Murja is a perfectly respectable age to get married.'

Liyah responded stiffly. 'I just think it's too young to throw away your independence.'

Sharif raised a brow. His mouth quirked. 'I've married a feminist?'

'Is that a problem?'

Sharif laid an arm across the back of the couch and it pulled the material of his shirt and waistcoat across his broad chest. Distracting Liyah. She cursed him, because he probably knew exactly what he was doing.

He answered, 'Not at all. I don't see how any woman can say she's *not* a feminist.'

Liyah's prickliness and scattered thoughts disappeared. She looked at him.

He said, 'Don't look so surprised. My mother was a strong woman, and if it hadn't been for her I would have had to spend even more time with my father.'

'How old were you when she died?'

Sharif didn't move a muscle, but Liyah sensed his reticence.

'Nine. It was a long time ago.'

Clearly they'd been close. Liyah felt a pang to think of how different her own life might have been if her mother hadn't died so young.

'So,' he repeated, 'why did you take your sister's place?'

Liyah hesitated at the prospect of telling Sharif the truth, but then reminded herself that he hadn't even cared which sister he married. 'Because she's in love with someone else and wants to marry him.'

'But you just said you think she's too young to give up her independence…isn't it a contradiction to approve of her marrying someone else?'

Liyah's conscience pricked. She *had* just contradicted herself—spectacularly. She felt like squirming. No one had ever questioned her this closely about anything. 'I just want her to be happy… But I'm afraid she'll be disappointed. Because love doesn't exist—or, if it does, it's a destructive force.'

'That's a very cynical view to have.'

'Something tells me that a man who is prepared to seduce a stranger the night before his arranged marriage doesn't exactly hold love in high esteem,' Liyah observed drily.

Sharif acknowledged that with a dip of his head. 'Touché.'

For a moment Liyah felt a heady rush of exhilaration. Here was a kindred spirit. Was that why she'd been so drawn to him on sight? Because she'd sensed an unconscious affinity? It would certainly help explain her uncharacteristic behaviour.

And yet, even though she recognised and welcomed the sense of affinity, the exhilaration faded to leave a hollow echo inside her to know he was as cynical as her.

'So, who hurt you?'

Liyah's breath stopped for a second at his question. She wondered if she'd heard correctly. 'Excuse me?'

'You're not innocent, but you're not experienced. So, whoever your lover was, he either hurt you badly enough to spark your cynicism or he merely confirmed it. And he didn't ensure that you were satisfied.'

Liyah wanted to slide under the chair and into the floor. Had it been so obvious? No wonder he didn't want to repeat the experience.

'You think you see a lot.'

He practically smirked. 'I know I do. It is a skill honed over many years.'

The need to know how and why he'd developed such a skill hovered on Liyah's tongue, but before she could say a word there was a sound and they both blinked, as if taken by surprise at the way their conversation had engrossed them.

Liyah looked to the door, where a middle-aged gentleman stood. She hadn't even known anyone else was in the place, but it was so vast she wasn't surprised.

Sharif stood up. 'Liyah, I'd like you to meet Thomas Burke, the house manager here.'

Liyah stood up and met the man halfway. Shaking his hand, she smiled, feeling suddenly shy.

'Mrs Marchetti, it's a pleasure to welcome you to New York.'

Sharif glanced at his watch and said, 'I have to go downtown for some meetings and to catch up on my calls. Thomas will show you around and take note of any dietary requirements. You should settle in, Liyah, I'll be back for dinner.'

Take note of any dietary requirements. As if she was literally an employee.

Which she pretty much was.

Sharif walked out, taking his jacket with him, and Liyah breathed out fully for the first time since they'd arrived at the apartment.

She dutifully followed Thomas around the different rooms and tried not to let her jaw drop too obviously. There were two dining rooms—informal and formal. A massive kitchen with its own elegant dining area. There was a gym, with a lap pool, and a media centre, complete with a cinema that could seat about fifty people.

There were numerous bedrooms.

She noticed that Thomas didn't show her into

Sharif's, but she was given a room just across the hall and it was show-stopping. Decorated in dark blues and greys, with a shag pile carpet, it was decadent and glamorous.

It had its own terrace and a dressing room, and en suite bathroom that was about as big as the hammam back in Taraq.

Thomas stood in the doorway, not a hint of curiosity about the fact that the new Mrs Marchetti and her husband were obviously not traditional man and wife showing on his face.

'As Mr Marchetti said, let me know if you have any specific dietary preferences and I'll pass them on to the chef.'

The chef!

Liyah balked. 'How many staff are here?'

Thomas calculated for a second. 'Daily, about three—the housemaid, the chef and myself. Then weekly there's a few more—the florist...people like that.'

Liyah had seen the gorgeous colourful blooms in the hall... Thomas was looking at her. She hadn't answered. 'Oh, sorry—nothing. No preferences. I eat anything.'

Thomas looked almost comically taken aback for a moment, and then he bowed ever so slightly and smiled. 'Very good. Dinner will be served at seven, and Mr Marchetti will be in the lounge for an aperitif at six-thirty. Just press the bell by your bed if you need anything in the meantime.'

Thomas left and Liyah investigated her space. Her luggage had been magically unpacked and put away, and she tried not to wince at how shabby her things looked in the pristine space.

She had sisters who wouldn't be caught dead in anything without a designer label, but that had just been one of the many differences between them and Liyah.

She explored the terrace, taking in the truly stupendous view. The sidewalk looked many miles below her, where people scurried like ants. The sky was bright blue and the air was sharp and cold. But there was no snow.

Liyah had never seen snow. It hadn't ever been that cold when she'd been in Europe.

Despite her sleep on the plane, Liyah felt weary. It had been a tumultuous couple of days. And this was supposedly her wedding night with her new husband. Except it was morning—daytime—and they were on the other side of the world. And he obviously had no intention of sleeping with her again.

Thoroughly discombobulated, and not wanting to dwell on the revelations of her new situation, Liyah took off her clothes and crawled into the enormous bed between sheets that felt like silk to the touch. She was asleep in seconds.

That evening Sharif looked out over the view of a lowering grey sky. He'd never really got used

to the cold winters in New York, but as this was
where he'd moved the headquarters of the Marchetti Group's operations after his father's death
he'd come to tolerate them.

Moving here from the main hub in Rome had
been his first step in breaking all ties with his
father's legacy. His first step in stamping out his
father's influence. The next steps would be the
final death knells and would wipe Domenico
Marchetti's name out of existence, reducing his
legacy to dust.

But even now, as he reminded himself of all
that was at stake and all that was to come, Sharif
couldn't focus. He was distracted. He'd been distracted all day. Thinking of *her*. His new wife.
The woman who was also his mysterious temptress from the oasis—who had lured him like a
siren and then kissed him like a novice.

But now he knew better. She'd been no novice.

She'd known exactly what she was doing at that
oasis and she'd taken him for a complete fool—

A sound from behind him brought his thoughts
to a stop. He turned around slowly. His wife stood
in the doorway. She looked hesitant. She was
wearing a long cream traditional Taraqi tunic.
V-necked, it dipped just low enough to show the
top of the curve of her breasts. She also wore
slim-fitting matching trousers and flat sandals.
He noticed there was still henna on her feet. If

this was a traditional marriage he would be taking her to his bed tonight.

A skewer of need twisted in Sharif's gut and he crushed it. This was *not* a traditional marriage and he would *not* be taking her to his bed. Ever again.

Her hair was down, curling wildly around her shoulders, parted in the middle to reveal the effortless beauty of her face. Those huge almond eyes. Wide, generous mouth, lush lips. High cheekbones.

Sharif could imagine her as a teenager, all coltish limbs and awkward grace. But now she was a grown woman, and he had seriously underestimated her.

'Would you like a drink?' He forced civility into his voice when he felt far from civil.

She nodded and walked in.

Sharif couldn't help but notice the soft sway of her breasts under the material of her tunic. *Dio.* She wasn't wearing a bra. Considering what he knew now, he suspected that was on purpose. Her talk of not needing money from him had been a cute deflection from her true nature.

'A soda and lime would be nice, thank you.'

So demure. So deceptive.

Sharif poured her drink, handed it to her, and then poured himself a Scotch.

She hovered, as if unsure what to do or where to go.

Her apparent reticence irritated him now. It was all an act. He cursed himself for not investigating her sooner. But he *had* investigated her sister, and nothing untoward had come back, so he'd just assumed she would be the same. A serious lapse in Sharif's usual attention to detail.

'Please, sit, Liyah. You don't need permission.'

Liyah sat on one of the couches, sending him a slightly inquisitive look, which he ignored.

Sharif chose a chair. Instead of demanding that she explain herself straight away, he decided to play dumb. 'Did you rest this afternoon?'

She nodded and took a sip of her drink. 'Yes, thank you.'

But Sharif knew he couldn't string this out—he was too angry. 'You don't have to thank me for everything. This is your home now too, and you're free to come and go. But...' He paused for a moment, watching her carefully. 'I will not tolerate the kind of behaviour you have displayed on your hedonistic jaunt around Europe over the last couple of years.'

Hedonistic jaunt.

Liyah had just taken a sip of her drink and she nearly choked, but she managed to swallow before she did.

She looked at her husband.

He'd seen the papers and the paparazzi photos. The hurt that she'd felt the first time she'd realised she'd been so betrayed felt fresh again. The fact that she wasn't similarly armed with information on Sharif made her feel very defenceless now. But then she told herself she was being paranoid.

'What exactly are you talking about?'

His mouth thinned. 'The nice little portfolio my assistant put together for me, featuring your various and myriad exploits last summer in Europe, mainly on the Côte d'Azur.'

She wasn't being paranoid. Liyah's insides cramped. 'Those pictures weren't—'

He cut in. 'Weren't what they looked like? Spare me the excuses, Liyah. It was pretty clear what they were—pictures of an entitled royal socialite living to excess. But I couldn't care less what you got up to, or that you seem to like to affect this act of faux innocence and naivety. What I do care about is that you do not repeat that behaviour while you are married to me. Luckily the pictures didn't get picked up by the wider gossip sites. And we're going to keep it that way. You won't be hooking up with any of your Eurotrash party friends while you're with me.'

Liyah felt sick. She could see the pictures in her mind's eye. Lolling on the deck of a massive yacht in the sparkling Mediterranean Sea drinking champagne. Falling out of famous nightclubs being held up by so-called friends. Shopping in the most famous shops and streets of Spain, Italy, Paris... You name it, she'd been there.

Except she hadn't.

Because the girl in those pictures hadn't been her.

The words to try and explain this to Sharif trembled on her tongue, but he was like a stone. Disgusted. Disapproving. And a need to protect herself rose up. She would only be with this man for a year at the most. He didn't deserve to know the real her—the woman far removed from those pictures.

And how could she defend herself when his first impression of her had been the wanton woman he'd met at the oasis, who had shown no hesitation in jumping into bed with a complete stranger? No wonder he believed the worst.

She forced the emotion out of her voice. 'You can rest assured that I won't be a liability while we're married.'

Thomas appeared in the doorway at that moment, with perfect timing, to announce dinner.

Liyah preceded Sharif out of the room and tried not to feel like a chastened child. But it was hard when she wanted to stamp her feet and tell him that he had it all wrong. The injustice made her breathless, but she felt a stronger need not to let him see the soft, vulnerable part of her that very few had ever seen.

* * *

To Liyah's relief, Sharif hadn't brought up those lurid paparazzi shots again over their deliciously cooked dinner of tender chicken and rice infused with herbs and spices. But it appeared that he wasn't prepared to let everything go.

He leant back now, a nearly empty wine glass in his hand, and looked at her. 'I believed that someone must have hurt you, but if anything it's more likely to have been the other way around. Who was he?'

Liyah kept her face expressionless, even as she sucked in a breath at the barb. He thought she'd been acting the whole time. Feigning her reticence and lack of experience.

An image came into her head. A young man— her age. Tall, handsome. Cheeky smile. Charming. Intelligent. How easily he'd swept her off her feet and made her believe that he was truly interested in her. How easily she'd let him breach barriers she'd never allowed anyone else to, so self-protective and distrustful.

But when she'd first arrived in Europe a couple of years ago she'd been hungry to experience this new world and be a modern, independent woman. So one night she'd allowed him the ultimate intimacy.

She hadn't told him she was a virgin, too embarrassed and shy, and eager to relieve herself of the burden of innocence. But when she'd tensed at the unexpected pain on penetration he'd stopped, a horrified look on his face, clearly not expecting a fellow university student of twenty-two to still be a virgin.

For a moment she'd thought he'd force himself on her, but he'd jumped up and hurled a string of profane insults instead. And then she'd discovered that she was the butt of a random drunken bet between him and his friends to see how quickly he could get her into bed. Apparently he'd won his bet.

After that Liyah could remember covering up with tomboyish clothes. Tying her hair back. Wearing her glasses all the time. Diminishing herself as much as possible to avoid sticking out on the university campus. Drawing attention.

And yet Sharif had just had to look at her and she'd forgotten the painful lessons she'd learnt in a heartbeat. Sheer instinct had overridden every rational bone in her body, proving that there was still a shameful hunger inside her, ready to expose her weakness for connection and intimacy at all costs. She'd learnt nothing. And this man wasn't about to believe what she had to say in her defence. So she would protect herself by playing to his low regard of her.

She pushed the hurt down and lifted her chin. 'He was nobody. I don't even remember his name.'

'I almost feel sorry for him.'

when usually the thought of coming back to an empty apartment was unappealing. But he'd been watching the clock since late afternoon. Texting his security team to see what Liyah was doing.

She'd gone to the New York Public Library and spent hours inside.

And now, as he walked into the living area and was confronted with the sight of Liyah sitting cross-legged on a chair, in sweat pants and a soft, clingy cashmere top, with her hair piled on her head, reading a book, he knew that something wasn't adding up.

But he didn't feel inclined to worry about it right then.

He leant against the doorframe. 'I didn't know you wore glasses.'

She looked up, startled. And as he watched, her cheeks flushed darker. It had an immediate effect on his blood, bringing it to the boil after simmering all day. It was getting harder to keep his sexual frustration under control.

The glasses suited her. They made her look serious. Seriously sexy. But, as if hearing his thoughts, she took them off.

She closed the book. 'I wasn't sure what time you'd be back…if you'd have had dinner. I'm not sure how this works.'

Sharif straightened up and walked into the room. Its soft lighting gave everything a golden glow, including her. She watched him approach and desire coiled tight in his body. He undid his tie, and the buttons on his waistcoat, aware of her eyes following his movements as if she couldn't help herself.

He sat down on a chair near hers and picked up her book from where she'd put it down. A weighty tome on the history of New York.

She said, a little defensively, 'I wanted to read up about the city.'

Sharif put the book down. 'Perfectly commendable.' Although annoyingly inconsistent with the kind of person he thought she was. Right now she looked about as far removed from a partying socialite as it was possible to get.

Sharif made a mental note to get his team to make a more thorough investigation into what she'd been doing in Europe, suddenly suspicious as to why she was behaving so differently.

'Have you eaten?' he asked.

She nodded. 'Paul, the chef, made me a delicious beef stew. There's loads left over if you're hungry.'

A pang caught Sharif unexpectedly in the chest. No one had ever worried about saving him food before.

He shook his head. 'I had take-out in the office.'

Liyah made a face. 'That's not very healthy.'

Sharif smiled mockingly. 'Concerned for my welfare, Liyah? I told you—I don't need a wife, except on paper.'

Those mesmerising green eyes sparked and narrowed. 'Don't worry. I won't concern myself with your wellbeing again.'

Sharif cursed himself for goading her. Before he did something he'd regret, he stood up and put his hands in his pockets. 'You should go to bed, Liyah, it's late. And we're going to be taking a flight to Paris tomorrow night.'

Liyah was still trying to control her heart, which had been racing since she'd seen Sharif in the doorway, looking sexily dishevelled. Jaw stubbled. He loomed over her now, and she scrambled up from the chair and moved to the window, putting some distance between them.

Whenever he was around it felt hard to breathe.

She felt prickly—because she'd been unprepared to see him again, even after a day apart. *Not* prickly because she'd felt a little abandoned. She didn't like the sensation that she was in control of so little. Not helped by Sharif's effect on her.

'I have no objection to going to Paris, but a bit of forewarning would be nice.'

A muscle in Sharif's jaw pulsed. But he said equably, 'I'll arrange for my assistant to forward you my schedule, so you know what's coming up.'

'Thank you.' Now she felt as if she was over-reacting.

Sharif shrugged minutely. 'No problem. I should have thought of it before now.'

'What's happening in Paris?'

'Some meetings with my brother and our team there, and there's an event to attend.'

'What kind of event?'

'A charity ball.' Sharif glanced at his watch. 'I have some more work to do this evening. The stylist will come tomorrow to make sure you have all you need for the trip.'

Liyah felt a spurt of relief that she wouldn't have to figure it out herself, but at the same time she felt indignation that he didn't trust her to pack the right things.

He turned and left the room, and Liyah's eyes were drawn helplessly to his fluid grace. All that taut energy. She turned around, disgusted with herself, and then groaned when she saw her reflection in the darkened window.

She imagined how Sharif had seen her just now. Hair piled up. Leisurewear. No make-up. Wearing glasses, reading a book. It was no wonder he didn't desire her any more. And that was fine with her.

Just fine.

Paris

'You like to be high up, don't you?'

Liyah couldn't keep the amused tone from her

voice as she looked around Sharif's Paris apartment. It was on the top floor of a stunning nineteenth-century building, with views from almost every window of the Eiffel Tower in the near distance. It had a terrace and an elegantly modern interior design.

'I appreciate a good view.'

Liyah turned around to face him. 'Yes, but how often do you actually look at it?'

'Has anyone ever told you that you ask a lot of questions?'

Liyah blanched as a nanny's voice came back into her head. *Always with the questions, Aaliyah. No one wants a princess who asks too many questions for a wife.*

She'd been about six, and even at that young age she'd decided that if she couldn't ask questions then she didn't want to be a princess, or anyone's wife.

'What is it?' Sharif's voice was sharp.

Liyah shook her head. 'Nothing—just a moment of déja-vu.'

He looked at his watch. 'I'm afraid I have to go straight to the office, but I'll take you to lunch in a few hours. You should get some rest.'

Liyah had slept on the plane—an overnight flight, bringing them into Paris early in the morning. She'd noticed that Sharif hadn't slept. He'd been on his laptop or his phone the whole time. He evidently didn't need sleep, like mere mortals.

'I'm okay. Actually, I might take a walk around…stretch my legs.'

Sharif shrugged. 'Whatever you want. One of the security team will go with you.'

Liyah opened her mouth to object, but shut it again when she saw the look on Sharif's face. It wasn't worth arguing. Even though she came from a royal family, they'd never been important or rich enough to merit serious protection. But she was at another level now.

He left the apartment, and after Liyah had freshened up she explored a little more, finding a media room and a gym with a lap pool. It looked very inviting, but she wanted to get out into the fresh air and see Paris again. It was one of her favourite cities.

She bundled up against the cool late winter breeze and set out to the Eiffel Tower, which was further away than she'd thought. An optical illusion.

When she reached it, she stood in the plaza among lots of other tourists milling around, and looked up at the majestic structure. Paris had been the first foreign city she'd visited after London, and she'd adored wandering around, getting lost in the *arrondissements*, sitting in cafés and lingering over coffee, watching the world go by.

You were lonely, though.

Liyah pushed the voice aside. *Not* lonely. Independent. Happy.

She saw her security man a few feet away, on his phone, his face towards her, his eyes hidden behind black shades.

Liyah went over. 'Is that Sharif?'

The man hesitated before nodding.

Liyah held out her hand, and he gave her the phone with clear reluctance. She said into it, 'Hello, Sharif.'

There was silence at the other end, and then a sigh. 'Yes, Liyah?'

'If you're so concerned about where I am and what I'm up to you should leave your stuffy meeting and come and see some sights for yourself.'

He had said he would meet her for lunch, but she didn't believe that. Anyway, she was used to occupying herself.

But then Sharif said, 'I'll meet you there. Wait for me.'

He terminated the call and Liyah handed back the phone, a little stunned. And excited. She turned away from the security guard, who pocketed his phone again and resumed his stony-faced position. Liyah tried but failed to block out the fluttery feeling in her belly.

Sharif saw her before she saw him. She was sitting on a low wall facing the Eiffel Tower. She was wearing jeans, Chelsea boots, and a dark green turtleneck under a leather bomber jacket with a sheepskin lining. Her hair was pulled up into a bun, with curling wayward strands framing her face. She also wore sunglasses. No different to many of the monied tourists around her, but a world apart at the same time.

She was drawing attention just sitting still. Her natural beauty too obvious to ignore. But she appeared not to notice. Before, Sharif would have immediately been cynical about that, believing that she was well aware of the attention she attracted. But now…he couldn't be sure.

He'd been right to investigate her more thoroughly. The fact that she'd flipped the tables on him *again* was becoming irritating in the extreme.

CHAPTER SEVEN

'How did you get a table here at such short notice?' Liyah asked, taking in the astounding views all around them from the ultra-exclusive restaurant in the Eiffel Tower. Then she rolled her eyes and answered herself. 'Stupid question, don't bother answering.'

She looked at Sharif, who was still in the three-piece suit that he'd changed into on the plane before landing. He looked as fresh as if he'd just woken from a ten-hour sleep.

The waiter came and took their orders. Even though they weren't near the top, they were still high enough that people looked like ants down below, milling around at the bottom of the tower.

Liyah said, 'I was only joking when I said that you should come. I didn't mean to break up your day.'

'I said I'd meet you for lunch.'

The waiter returned with white wine and poured two glasses. Sharif lifted his and said, *'Santé.'*

Liyah clinked her glass with his. *'Santé.'*

She took a sip, but was very aware of Sharif's gaze, which had turned calculating. She suddenly felt nervous and had no idea why.

He said nothing at first. Over a delicious starter of asparagus, and a main course of chicken breast, he lulled Liyah into a false sense of security by conducting a light conversation regarding her likes and dislikes—everything from movies to books and art.

Apparently he too enjoyed twisty dark thrillers, and he revealed a surprisingly nerdy interest in comic books.

He said, 'There were tons of them in my Scottish boarding school. I used to take piles of them and hide in one of the gardener's sheds, and get lost in them for hours. It was worth the punishment when the staff thought I'd run away.'

Liyah gasped. 'They punished you?'

Sharif's mouth flattened. 'It wasn't a good place.'

He put down his glass of wine and leant forward.

Liyah was still thinking of that dark-haired young boy, being subjected to some awful humiliation, far from home, griefstruck, so when Sharif asked, almost idly, 'When were you going to tell me that it isn't you in those paparazzi shots?' Liyah almost missed it.

Her skin went clammy. Maybe she'd heard wrong. She'd been distracted. 'What did you say?'

'You heard me. It wasn't you in those paparazzi pictures.'

'How do you know?'

'Because I looked at them properly after I realised you weren't behaving like a spoiled socialite. Far from it.'

Liyah felt as if a layer of her skin had been stripped back. Incredibly vulnerable.

Sharif sat back. 'What I want to know is why you wouldn't tell me the truth when I confronted you about it? Why pretend to be something you're not?'

Liyah admitted defeat. 'The day you brought it up…it seemed easier just to let you believe what you wanted. I barely knew you. Everything had happened so fast.' She avoided his eye and plucked at her napkin. 'I guess it felt like a kind of armour. I wasn't ready to let you know who I was, and you didn't seem inclined to want to know.' She looked at him. 'You were too busy telling me that I was pretty much a bought companion, purely for public appearances.'

Sharif had the grace to look slightly discomfited. 'Yes, well… I was still coming to terms with the fact that *you*, the mystery woman from the oasis, and my new wife were one and the same. And you have to admit that your behaviour that night—*our* behaviour,' he amended, 'didn't exactly dissuade me from believing the worst.'

'That was part of it too,' Liyah admitted. 'I didn't think you'd believe me.'

'So, if you weren't tripping on and off yachts and spending up a storm and falling out of night-clubs, what *were* you doing?'

Sharif's gaze was direct and unwavering. Liyah tipped up her chin. 'I do like to dance, and I did go to nightclubs.'

'But, like most people, you probably managed not to fall out of them. Who's the girl in the pictures?'

'She's a Middle Eastern model. One of my sisters spotted that she looked like me. Same hair. Height…'

'She's totally different. She's about half your weight and she has no breasts.'

He glanced at her chest, making Liyah all too conscious of her larger than fashionable breasts under the soft fabric of her sweater. And her nipples were reacting to his look right now, growing hard, tingling…

She said in a strangled voice, 'I think we look totally different too, but she worked for what my father wanted and so he paid her to behave like a spoiled socialite and then tipped the press off that it was me.'

Sharif—thankfully—lifted his gaze back up to Liyah's face. 'Why would he do that?'

Liyah tried to ignore the familiar pang of hurt. 'Because telling people I was misbehaving all around Europe was preferable to admitting that I had left Taraq to try and live an independent life, which is all I've ever wanted.'

'What were you doing?'

Liyah's heart was beating fast. She hated it that it mattered to her what Sharif thought. 'I got a place at Oxford. I did a Master's in Economic and Social History over two years.'

'A Master's? Had you done an undergraduate course?'

Liyah shook her head. 'No, I'd studied for the Baccalaureate with a tutor in Taraq, and I did an interview, and they accepted me.' Liyah's mouth twisted. 'I'm sure being an international student with ready funds helped.'

Sharif shook his head. 'They're more discerning than that at Oxford. How many languages do you speak?'

'Arabic—obviously. English, French, and passable Italian and Spanish.'

'And if you were here for the summer holidays, and not falling out of clubs and onto yachts, what were you doing?'

'One summer I worked in a vineyard in France, picking grapes, and I also worked in the library at Oxford.'

'And your family were *angry* that you were doing that?'

'My father is conservative. He doesn't approve

of my desire for independence. To be honest, I didn't expect them even to notice that I was gone.'

Liyah looked directly at Sharif, daring him to pity her. This wasn't about self-pity—even if her family's disregard for her had brought pain.

'My father turned his back on me a long time ago—after my mother died. He moved on with his other wives and children.'

Sharif said tautly, 'That's why I have no intention of having children. I've only known a father to be a destructive force, and I wouldn't wish that on anyone else.'

Before, Liyah would have agreed with Sharif, but something rogue made her say now, 'We're not our fathers.'

'Do you want children?'

In all honesty, Liyah wasn't sure any more. 'I want a life of freedom and independence. I don't see how children fit into that. And I'm aware that's selfish.'

Sharif shook his head. 'It's not selfish to want what most people take for granted. You'll have all the freedom you want within a year at the latest, Liyah. You'll be wealthy enough to do whatever you want, wherever you want.'

Once again, instead of relief, Sharif's words precipitated an ominous ache inside her. It was the same hollow sensation she'd felt when he'd laid out so succinctly that he didn't want a relationship...

There was a low beeping sound and Sharif picked up his phone, which had been face-down on the table. Liyah blinked and looked around. She'd been so caught in the bubble of Sharif's focus that she hadn't noticed that the restaurant had emptied around them.

He was speaking into his phone now. 'Okay, we'll see you there.' He put his phone away and said, 'That was my brother Nikos. He and his wife Maggie will also be at the charity ball tonight, so you'll get to meet them.'

'They live in Paris?'

Sharif nodded as he gestured to one of the staff for the bill. 'They also have a house in Ireland, and they spend a lot of time there. Maggie's Scottish, but was brought up in Ireland. They have a son, Daniel, who is about eight months old, and Maggie is pregnant with their second child.'

Liyah squinted at Sharif. 'So, you have a nephew and another one, or a niece, on the way?'

Sharif made a face. 'It's a girl, apparently. And my other brother Maks has just announced that his wife is pregnant too.' He stood up. 'I'm afraid I have to go back to the office, but my driver can take you to the apartment. We'll leave for the ball at seven p.m.'

Liyah stood up too, still absorbing the fact that Sharif's brothers seemed to be well on their way to creating families. Surely if they had only got married for appearances' sake, like her and Sharif, they wouldn't be actively having babies?

As they walked back outside Sharif put on his overcoat and sunglasses. Liyah saw the women nearby—and the men—doing double takes. And then third takes. She rolled her eyes.

Sharif said again, 'Take my car.'

Liyah said, 'It's okay. I'll walk back to the apartment.'

'Suit yourself. A stylist will bring some dresses by for you to choose from. It's a black tie event.'

Liyah was turning away when Sharif called her name. She stopped. He came and stood in front of her. She couldn't see his eyes behind the dark shades.

He said, 'Don't let them touch your hair. Leave it loose.'

Liyah's heart hitched. 'Why? It's so messy—'

'Just…don't touch it.'

He turned and walked away, long strides putting distance between them within seconds. Liyah looked after him, afraid of the very tender sensation she could feel near her heart because he wanted her to look like…*her*. Especially after what she had just revealed—the truth about her European trip. The truth of who she was.

A bit of an academic nerd. Someone who wanted to travel. And read. And be independent. Someone most of her family didn't really care about.

The fact that Sharif had realised himself that she wasn't the girl in the photos had hit Liyah in a very deep and secret place, where she hid her hurts and vulnerabilities. It was all too seductive to read a deeper meaning into Sharif's comment about leaving her hair in its natural unstyled state.

But then Liyah castigated herself and turned abruptly and walked away in the opposite direction. She was being ridiculous. There was no deep or hidden meaning in Sharif wanting her to leave her hair alone. Absolutely none. No matter how much she might want there to be.

And *that* was something that she definitely was not going to acknowledge.

That evening, Liyah took a deep breath as she stood in front of the mirror. It was crazy—she knew she was a princess—but increasingly she actually *felt* like a princess.

The dress was strapless, with a sweetheart neckline and low back. How it stayed up was a feat of engineering and bodice work that Liyah didn't understand, but it felt secure. It was in the most delicate shade of blush pink, almost nude with a golden embroidered overlay. It had a cinched-in waist and a full, long tulle skirt and a small train that made it dramatic without being too loud.

The dress shimmered and glistened when she moved, and with it she wore gold hued high heels.

A very nice girl had appeared with the stylist, to do her hair and make-up, and the stylist had brought her pink diamond earrings and a matching bracelet.

The women had left not long ago, and now Liyah looked at herself again. Her hair was down, as requested, and the girl had brushed it until it flowed like ripples of silk over her shoulders, the unruliness tamed somewhat.

There was a knock on the door. Liyah's heart slammed against her breastbone. She opened it, and her eyes widened as she took in Sharif in a white tuxedo jacket, with a white shirt and black bow tie. He looked dark and sexy.

There was silence. And then Sharif said, 'You look...stunning, Liyah.'

She felt shy. 'Thank you. So do you.'

They went down to the foyer of the building, where the concierge held open the door and their driver was waiting, helping Liyah into one side of the car while Sharif got into the other.

The dress had a thigh-high slit and Liyah held the edges together over her thigh for the duration of the journey. Not that Sharif would even notice if she stripped naked, she was sure.

When they arrived at a seriously opulent-looking hotel, Sharif got out and came around, opening her door. He helped her out and kept hold of her hand, leading her onto the red carpet.

They stopped for the ubiquitous pictures. Liyah

tried not to flinch every time a flash went off, wondering if she'd ever get used to it.

Beside her, Sharif said, *sotto voce*, 'That was one of the first things to make me suspect that perhaps there was more to you than you'd told me.'

'What was that?'

'Your lack of ease in front of the photographers. I noticed it at the Met.'

She looked up and met his gaze. A moment passed between them—a sense of affinity, delicate and ephemeral. His eyes moved to her mouth and he lifted a brow in question. Liyah knew what he was asking and she gave one tiny nod, her skin prickling all over in anticipation.

His head descended and his mouth brushed hers, light enough to tease, but strong enough to make her move closer, making a small sound. Her free hand went to his chest and he caught it there.

Then he pulled back. The world was a deafening clatter of sound and flashing lights.

'Mr Marchetti, another kiss, please!'

'Princess Aaliyah—over here. Who are you wearing?'

Liyah felt dizzy, but she watched as Sharif calmly faced the photographers and said, 'Mrs Marchetti is wearing Elie Saab couture.'

He moved forward and Liyah followed unsteadily, trying to get her hammering heart back into a normal rhythm. He'd barely kissed her, and it had been purely for the cameras, but she was reduced to jelly. What would happen if he kissed her in private?

Not going to happen, she reminded herself.

By the time they reached the main reception she was marginally under control again.

Sharif stopped suddenly and said something in Italian that she didn't catch. Then he turned to her, pulling his phone out. 'There was something I wanted to show you before we left the apartment, but I got distracted.'

Liyah's heart sped up again. Had she distracted him? She hoped so, because he distracted *her* all the time.

He handed her his phone. It was a press release, headed with the Marchetti Group's logo.

We accept the apology from Celebrity! Magazine, which published photos of a woman last year, claiming them to be of Princess Aaliyah Binte Rashad Mansour.

It was, in fact, a model called Ameera Sayam.

Celebrity! Magazine have agreed to donate an undisclosed amount of money to a charity chosen by the Marchetti Group, and extend their apologies for having caused Mrs Aaliyah Marchetti any distress.

The words swam ominously in front of Liyah's eyes and she quickly blinked. Until that moment she hadn't realised how hurtful it was that her own father had betrayed her in such a way. And now Sharif had gone out of his way to clear her name.

She handed back his phone. 'Thank you...you didn't have to do that.' Her voice was husky.

'I did, actually. Your reputation now affects me and the Marchetti Group.'

Liyah's emotions shrivelled. He'd done it for pragmatic reasons. Not for *her*. 'Of course.'

A waiter approached and Sharif took two glasses of champagne, handing Liyah one. She avoided his eye and took a quick sip, hoping he wouldn't notice anything. What was it about this man? She'd been more aware of her emotions in the past couple of weeks than she had her whole life.

And of your desires, pointed out a wicked inner voice.

Sharif took her hand again and led her into the crowd. She'd never seen so many beautiful people in her life. Women in shimmering dresses like hers. Blinging with jewels... The smell of perfume was almost overwhelming...

And then from behind them Liyah heard a voice.

'There they are! Sharif!'

Sharif turned around and Liyah followed him to see a man approaching. He was as tall as Sharif and very dark, with thick curly hair.

He was also astonishingly good-looking, with a classical beauty that reminded Liyah of a Greek statue. She recognised Nikos from the pictures she'd seen on the internet.

And the woman beside him. Tall—as tall as Liyah, if not taller—and very pale, with golden russet hair piled high, huge blue eyes.

She looked at Liyah and exclaimed, 'You must be Aaliyah!' She stuck out a hand. 'I'm Maggie. It's so nice to meet you.'

Liyah instinctively relaxed. Maggie was so friendly and open that it was impossible not to smile.

She shook her hand. 'It's Liyah, please—only my father calls me Aaliyah, and that's not a good thing.'

Maggie shook her hand and widened her eyes even more. She leant forward and whispered, 'Say no more. I understand all about Daddy issues. And as for these two...' Maggie gestured with her head towards Sharif and Nikos, who were watching them.

Liyah stifled a giggle. Nikos was rolling his eyes, but a smile played around his mouth as he wrapped an arm around Maggie's waist and pulled her to his side, whispering something in her ear that made her blush. It was then that Liyah noticed the bump under the form-fitting silk of her beautiful black evening dress.

'Congratulations,' she said.

Maggie put a hand on her neat bump and made a face. 'Thanks. It won't be easy, having two under two, but I like the idea of Daniel having a sibling close to his own age. I was an only child, and I always wanted brothers and sisters.'

Liyah was tempted to mention the fact that having a lot of siblings didn't exactly spell happy families...

'Liyah, this is Nikos.'

Sharif was introducing her to his brother. Liyah shook his hand, shyer than she'd been with Maggie. Nikos was smiling, and she could see how charming he was, but she could also detect that Marchetti steeliness.

These two were so clearly in love that Liyah felt bad for having entertained cynical doubts. She was very aware of the chasm between her and Sharif. Which was crazy, because love had no place for them.

Maggie was easy to talk to, and refreshingly normal in a world that Liyah barely recognised any more. She noticed that Sharif was tense around Nikos, but also how he couldn't help smiling at whatever Nikos said. She sensed that Sharif wanted to let his guard down, but wouldn't. Or couldn't.

They gradually moved closer to a central ballroom, where waltz music was playing. Maggie nudged her husband. 'You should ask Liyah to dance, Nikos—after all, we never got to celebrate the wedding.' She sent a look to Sharif, who just arched a brow.

Liyah was embarrassed, but before she knew how to respond Nikos was bowing before her and saying, 'If you would do me the honour, I'd love to have this dance.'

Relieved by the distraction, and wondering how much these two knew about the reality of her marriage with Sharif, Liyah put her hand in her brother-in-law's and let him lead her onto the dance floor. It was something of a respite to spend time with a man who didn't affect her so acutely. Who didn't look at her and make her skin feel tight and hot.

Nikos was a good dancer, fluid and strong. And she breathed out and let him take control.

He said above her head, 'That bad, eh…?'

She looked up. 'Excuse me?'

He winked. 'I heard that sigh of relief. And I know how tough it is spending time with Sharif, so I don't envy you.'

Immediately Liyah felt defensive. 'He's really not that bad.'

At all.

Nikos looked at her and she blushed. 'You… you do know? That the marriage isn't…'

'All I know,' he said diplomatically, 'is that I think you'll be good for him. He works too hard and he's too serious. I'd imagine that any adjustment in his life to accomodate someone else is a good thing.'

'He's told me you didn't grow up together?'

Nikos made a face. 'No, our beloved father didn't approve of us half-brothers actually getting to know one another. He had plans for us all in the business, and was counting on us competing against one another to keep the Marchetti Group on its toes. The fact that he wouldn't approve of us working together is something that makes things even sweeter now. Sharif was the one who pointed out to Maks and I that it was *our* legacy to protect.' Nikos shook his head 'But after what happened to him and his mother, I don't know how he didn't destroy it all at the first opportunity.'

'You wouldn't have minded?'

Nikos grimaced. 'I didn't care about much until I met Maggie again and knew I had a son. Now everything is changed.' He looked at Liyah and smiled. 'I blame my wife for the fact that I can't seem to keep anything to myself these days.'

Liyah smiled too. 'She's very sweet.'

Nikos looked over her head, presumably at his wife, and said, 'Yes she is.' And then, in an ominous voice, 'Incoming—behind you. I warn you now: the man is a terrible dancer.'

Nikos disappeared into the crowd just as Sharif appeared in her eyeline. He was glowering after his brother. They stood in the middle of the dance floor, with couples moving around them.

Sharif took Liyah's hand and moved to walk off, but she dug her heels in and hissed, 'It's the middle of the song.'

Sharif faced her. 'I told you I don't do this sort of thing.'

Liyah stepped close to him. Lifted her hands. For a moment Sharif looked so like a petulant little boy that she had to bite back a laugh. But then he muttered something and took her into his arms.

Instantly flames raced along Liyah's veins. Her core grew heavy and hot with desire. Sharif didn't have his brother's fluidity, it was true, but he moved with competent grace for such a big man.

Liyah looked up. 'Why do you hate dancing so much? You're not as bad as—' She cut herself off at Sharif's sharp look.

'Nikos oversharing again? Marriage and fatherhood have turned his brain soft.'

When he didn't say anything else, Liyah prompted, 'Well…?'

Sharif sighed. 'My father made me go to the Bal des Débutantes, here in Paris.'

'I know of it… I didn't go, but my sisters did.'

Liyah felt the familiar prickle of shame and tried to ignore it. The Bal des Débutantes was an invitation-only exclusive event, designed to introduce prominent young men and women of the world to society. Obviously she hadn't been deemed prominent enough by her family.

Sharif said, 'You were lucky. My father and I were both invited. Except my father didn't turn up. I missed the waltz class before the event and I was the only *cavalier* at the ball who didn't know how to dance. Throw in the fact that my father was reaching nuclear levels of press coverage at the time, and my mixed race heritage among the blue-eyed Princes of Europe made me stand out like a sore thumb... It didn't end well.'

Liyah's eyes widened. 'You got into a scrap?'

Sharif lifted the hand holding hers and pointed at a scar by his jaw.

Liyah reached out and ran her finger along the small indentation.

The moment Liyah's finger touched Sharif's skin an electric jolt went right down to his solar plexus. He stopped moving. She looked up at him, eyes huge. Her hair flowed over her shoulders, marking her out amongst all the other women with their complicated up-dos and overdone faces.

He didn't know what had compelled him to tell her to leave her hair down.

Yes, you do. You wanted to see her again as you saw her that night. Naked. Wild.

He shoved the provocative thought aside.

Once again she made everyone else pale in

comparison. She was vibrant. Full of an earthy sensuality that called to him on such an urgent and deep level that Sharif knew he was fighting a losing battle.

She barely had to touch him and he burned. He felt volatile, and it hadn't been helped by seeing Nikos and Maggie.

Being around his brothers, and now their wives, always put him on edge, left him filled with mixed emotions. Protectiveness, regret, affection... But also a strong instinct not to trust—and guilt. Because he hadn't told them everything he was planning.

Just seeing Liyah dancing with Nikos, smiling at whatever he was saying, had made the darkness inside him lash and roar, even when he knew for a fact that Nikos had eyes only for Maggie. He'd learnt not to test Nikos's loyalty in that regard, and now, with Maggie pregnant again, they inhabited a place that Sharif could not understand.

Seeing them so happy brought back painful echoes of his relationship with his mother. Her unconditional love and his feeling of security. Something that he'd told himself he would never need again, because the pain of losing it had been so great.

Sharif gritted his jaw. He really wasn't in the mood for these introspective thoughts. And yet here was Liyah, her huge green eyes looking up at him and making him feel as if she was seeing all the way down to where he kept his darkness hidden.

He'd noticed the emotion in her eyes when he'd shown her the press release about those paparazzi photos claiming to be of her. He knew damn well that he could have left it alone…that his comment about her reputation hadn't been entirely true—those photos had barely made a dent in the mainstream gossip columns. But he'd seen how much it had affected her when she'd told him about it, and he'd wanted to avenge her. So he'd instructed his legal team to extract an apology and a retraction from the magazine or force them to face a lawsuit.

They'd issued the press release within hours.

Sharif was aware of the song coming to an end and the sense of exposure mixed with those other volatile emotions in his gut boiled over. He needed to shut out the voices and the swirling thoughts and refocus. And he knew only one way to do that.

Stop denying himself. Stop denying them both.

He led Liyah off the dance floor, his blood pounding. They were almost at the main entrance when he felt her pulling on his hand. He stopped, looked at her.

She said, 'I know you don't like to hang around, but we literally just got here.'

Sharif felt drunk with lust. The light made her

skin gleam dark golden. The swells of her breasts above her bodice were a provocation he had no intention of resisting any longer. He'd forgotten why he'd ever thought it would be a good idea *not* to sleep with his wife.

He felt it in her too. She trembled whenever he touched her. Even now a blush was rising into her cheeks, staining them darker.

She said, 'Why are you looking at me like that?'

'I don't think this is working.'

She frowned. 'You don't think what isn't working?'

But Sharif was striding through the lobby of the hotel now, cutting a swathe through the throng of guests, Liyah's hand clamped firmly in his.

Liyah said from behind him, 'What about Nikos and Maggie? Don't we need to say goodbye? Don't you have people to meet?'

'Nikos can look after it. I'll send him a text.'

They walked outside and a valet scrambled to call Sharif's car and driver around. He felt Liyah shiver beside him and took off his jacket then put it on her.

He texted Nikos.

We've left. Will you cover for me?

He got a text back almost straight away.

Of course. Welcome to my world, brother.

There was a winking emoji, and then a laughing crying emoji.

Sharif scowled and shoved his phone back in his pocket. This, with Liyah, was nothing like what Nikos had gone through with Maggie. For a start, she'd had Nikos's son—when he'd met her again, he'd been a father.

Sharif felt desperate. Almost feral. Things he never usually allowed himself to feel. He was always so careful to show the world that he was not his wayward father. Or his playboy brother. But he didn't have a playboy brother any more. Right now he was channelling the Marchetti rebelliousness all by himself and he couldn't care less.

He wanted his wife.

CHAPTER EIGHT

LIYAH ABSORBED THE heat and scent from Sharif's jacket as the car pulled to a smooth stop beside them. He opened the door and she got in. She didn't know what was going on with him, but she desperately resisted the temptation to believe that the heated look in his eyes meant something.

They joined the crazy Paris traffic and Liyah said nothing at first. Waiting to see if Sharif would elaborate. But he was silent. Brooding.

Eventually Liyah had to break the growing tension. 'Um…what you said about something not working…what did you mean?'

Sharif turned to look at her, snapping out of his brooding mood. He lounged back against the side of the car. Liyah had never seen him like this. It intimidated her as much as it excited her. There was something careless about him. No… Something reckless. Dangerous.

'I meant that I don't think our current arrangement is working.'

The driver put up the privacy shield between the front and the back seats.

Liyah's stomach plummeted. She'd asked too many questions. She didn't fit into his world. She didn't look like those other effortlessly soignée women. He didn't want to dance. Not with her, anyway.

And why was her first reaction dismay?

Terrified he'd see how much he'd got to her, Liyah said stiffly, 'I think you're right. Obviously neither of us are really suited to this…arrangement—'

'I don't mean that—' Sharif interrupted her, but then broke off abruptly. He cursed.

Liyah realised the car had stopped moving, they were back at his apartment.

Before she could try to figure out what he *had* meant he was out of the car, opening her door and reaching for her, taking her hand and leading her into the building. When they were in the elevator he didn't let go of her hand. Still he didn't say anything.

Electricity crackled in the air between them. She was afraid to look at him, or put a name to it, or think about what it meant. But she could feel it in her gut. Desire. The flames were getting loose and licking at her insides. But what if she was wrong? What if—?

The elevator doors opened and Sharif led her into the apartment's foyer. The door closed behind her and Sharif let her hand go. She wobbled a little in her heels. Why was she out of breath all of a sudden?

Feeling incredibly nervous, she started to babble. 'I liked Nikos and Maggie. They're genuinely in love, aren't they?'

Sharif's expression was stark. He looked at her as if he'd never seen her before and then he said, 'I don't know much about love—but I know about *this*.'

Liyah frowned. 'About—?'

But her words were cut off when Sharif clamped his hands on her waist and pulled her into his body. All the air left her chest.

'This marriage in name only is not working.'

The look in his eye was explicit. His body was hard. His heart hammered under her hands, which were splayed across his chest. Liyah opened her mouth and then shut it again. The flames of desire licked higher. But even as they did, and as she became aware of the full meaning behind Sharif's declaration, she felt the need to resist.

'Are you sure that's a good idea?'

'I want my wife.' He growled the words.

It took a second for her to absorb that fact. To acknowledge how badly she'd wanted him to want her. How much it had flayed her inside to think that one night had been enough for him.

Then it sank in. Stark. Unvarnished.

I want my wife.

This was how he did it. No romance. He hadn't even said *I want you*. She was a commodity to him. He just wanted to scratch an itch—she was no different from his other lovers. Maybe seeing his brother with his wife had made him realise that he was missing convenient sex in his convenient marriage.

That suspicion made something close down inside Liyah.

She took a step back, dislodging Sharif's hands. 'Well, I don't think I'm prepared to renegogiate the parameters of this arrangement just because you want someone to warm your bed. I'm sure you have plenty of contacts you can call to alleviate your…urges.'

Deep inside, Liyah wondered what on earth she was saying. She was willingly pushing him into another woman's bed! But he'd never been hers in the first place. Not really. No matter how serendipitous or magical that night at the oasis had felt.

'I told you—I don't need any adverse press at this time.' He took a step towards her.

Panic at his proximity and her own weakness made Liyah put out a hand as if to ward him off. *Or grab him and bring him closer?* teased a sly inner voice.

She dropped her hand. 'So now I'm convenient not just for a marriage but also to scratch a physical itch?'

He took another step closer. His scent wrapped

around her like a siren call. Woody and oriental.
Infinitely seductive. She wanted to close her eyes,
breathe him in until she was dizzy.

He made a sound like a strangled laugh. 'Believe me, there's nothing "convenient" about how
you make me feel.'

Panic spiked. 'I don't mind if you want to take
someone else to bed. I won't say anything.'

He came closer, as if she hadn't spoken. Liyah
felt as if she was under water. His hands were
opening his jacket that was still on her and pushing it apart, over her shoulders and down her
arms. It fell to the floor at her feet with a muted
swish of fabric.

He said, almost to himself, 'The problem is
that I don't want anyone else. I only want you.'

You. Not *my wife.* Her. Liyah.

Treacherously, she felt her defences weaken.

Up close, he still towered over her, even in
heels. His jaw was dark with stubble. He was so
broad that he blocked everything else out.

And then he said, 'You really wouldn't mind?'

Liyah couldn't think straight. 'Wouldn't mind
what?'

'If I slept with another woman?'

A raging hungry beast reared up inside her,
and his scent and proximity made her defences
crumble to dust. She had an image of him at the
oasis, watching her emerge from the water, hold-

ing his hand out to her. Something very elemental moved through her.

This man was hers.

And right then she couldn't remember why it was so important to fight that.

'I would mind.'

Had she growled as she'd said that? She couldn't be sure, but she didn't care, because Sharif had his hands on her waist again and was tugging her towards him. It was only when their bodies touched that she realised she was shaking from the need overflowing inside her.

He went still. 'This doesn't change anything, Liyah. We're just letting our mutual chemistry burn out or else it'll drive us crazy. But that's all it is. It doesn't change what this marriage is.'

Not a marriage. A business arrangement.

'I know,' Liyah said, hoping she didn't sound too desperate. 'That's fine with me.'

She didn't want anything more either. She wanted her freedom. Independence. She certainly didn't want to risk her heart after a lifetime of learning that those who were meant to love you most either left you or rejected you. Or asked you to sacrifice your freedom for theirs.

This had nothing to do with emotions. It was desire. Physical. She could handle that.

To make sure he understood, she said, 'I want you, Sharif.'

As if a switch had been flicked, he muttered

something guttural and dug his hands into her hair, clasping her head, tipping her face up to his. Liyah gripped his arms and his muscles bunched under her palms. Her legs nearly gave way and she had to lock them to stay standing.

When his mouth covered hers electricity shot into her veins and straight to every erogenous point. She was suddenly ravenous, reaching up and straining to get closer. There were too many clothes in the way. She scrabbled for Sharif's waistcoat, pushing it off, dislodging his hands. Then his bow-tie and shirt.

When his chest was bare she pulled back and put her hands on him. He was warm and vital. The hair tickled her palms. His heart was thudding heavily. She felt drunk. Even though she'd barely touched her champagne earlier.

'You... I want to see you, Liyah.'

She turned around and pulled her hair over her shoulder, presenting him with her back. He pulled down her zip, his fingers stopping just above her buttocks. The dress loosened around her chest. Sharif came close behind her. She shivered when his bare chest met her back and his arms went around her, his hands cupping and measuring the weight of her breasts. She moaned with need, her head falling back against his shoulder.

He caught her jaw, tipped her face up so that his mouth could meet hers as he found and caught a nipple between his fingers, lightly pinching and rolling it until Liyah couldn't breathe with her need. She twisted in his arms, facing him again, her hands scrabbling for his belt, undoing it, opening a button, pushing his trousers and briefs down over his hips.

They were still standing in the foyer of the apartment. They'd barely moved two feet. But she didn't even notice. She took his rigid flesh in her hand, feeling the size and weight of him, hearing his sharp sucked-in breath, revelling in a momentary feeling of power.

He took her hand away. She looked up and quivered inwardly at the expression on his face.

'No time to play. I need you now.'

He backed her up until her shoulders hit the door with a soft thud. The wood was cool against her heated flesh. He crowded her and she revelled in it, wrapping her arms around his neck, rubbing her breasts against his chest.

She felt curiously emotional in the midst of this onslaught of sensation. She'd thought she'd never see him again after that night at the oasis. And then there'd been the shock of discovering he was her husband, and the belief that he didn't want her again.

But that was all incinerated to dust now, under his mouth. She squeezed her eyes shut to avoid him seeing anything of her feelings.

After a deep, drugging kiss, he broke away to press his mouth against her skin, her shoulder, her neck, and then down. He lifted her breast and cupped it so that he could zero in on her throbbing nipple, sucking and pulling the taut peak into his mouth, nipping with his teeth until Liyah was squirming, her every nerve-ending on fire.

Suddenly Sharif reared back and said throatily, 'Put your legs around me.'

Liyah kicked off her shoes, and when he lifted her up she locked her legs around his hips. The centre of her body came into contact with his, the flimsy lace of her underwear no barrier. She bit her lip, fighting not to beg because she knew that he was going to ease the burning ache in her core right here, right now.

He reached between them and she heard a faint rip. Her underwear. She didn't care. He guided the head of his erection to her centre, to where she was weeping with need. He looked at her as he teased her, lubricating his own body with the slick evidence of her desire.

And then, just when she thought she could take no more, he thrust deep, stealing her breath and her sanity. She was so primed that it took only a few deep, hard strokes to push her over the edge, and then her body clamped around Sharif's as he found his own release, his hips jerking in the aftermath of a storm so fast and intense they couldn't move for long moments.

Slowly Liyah began to put the shattered pieces of herself back together. She became aware of

Sharif's arm around her waist. His other hand was by her head, against the door. His face was buried in her neck, his breath uneven. Warm. Their hearts were pounding. Skin slick with perspiration.

Sharif lifted his head slowly. Liyah couldn't look away. She was aware that she'd never been more exposed, but she couldn't seem to care.

To her surprise, Sharif caught a piece of wayward hair and tucked it behind her ear. He said, 'Okay?'

She felt emotional again. She nodded quickly in a bid to distract him. To distract herself. 'Fine.'

When Sharif put her down gently, Liyah winced at the loss of connection. Her dress was ruched up to her waist and the top had fallen down, baring her breasts. Her underwear was strewn on the ground, as were her bag, Sharif's jacket and shirt and tie. Her shoes...

She pulled her dress up and bent to pick up her underwear. When she reached for the shoes Sharif took her hand and pulled her up.

'Leave them.'

He'd pulled his trousers up, but the button was still open. He looked thoroughly disreputable and dangerous, and Liyah's over-stimulated body pulsed back into life.

He tugged her behind him. She followed on legs like jelly, holding her dress up. 'Where are we going?'

He looked back at her and smiled wickedly. 'To continue discussing this renegotiation.'

Sharif stood looking down at the sleeping form of his wife for a long moment. She was sprawled on her front, one arm raised. He could see the plump flesh of one breast. Her lush bottom. Those long legs that had wrapped around him like a vice, holding him, pulling him so deep inside her that he'd seen stars.

His blood ran thickly in his veins in an overload of pleasure. He'd never experienced this after sex.

Liar.

He made a face to acknowledge the fact that he had. Once before. With the same woman.

The confirmation that her effect on him was still as potent was disturbing. Sex for him was usually a momentary thing, a passing release of energy. This was something else. Something he didn't want to investigate.

Because surely it would burn out.

It was nothing more than extraordinary chemistry.

He assured himself that he was merely taking advantage of an unprecedented situation—the fact that he wanted his convenient wife. If anything, not having to feign intimacy would help his cause. And, more importantly, it would defuse her ability to distract him.

But then Sharif became aware that he was still standing there, captivated by his sleeping wife. So much for not being distracted. He'd been due at a meeting half an hour ago.

With a scowl marring his features, and his body resisting leaving her behind, Sharif left the bedroom.

When Liyah woke she felt as if she was floating in a soft silken ocean. Every limb was heavy and utterly relaxed. There was a hum in her blood. A hum of satisfaction. But also of…hunger.

Her eyes snapped open as a rush of X-rated memories assailed her from last night. Sharif bringing her to his room, stripping her bare before stripping off his remaining clothes. Laying her on the bed and spreading her legs so that he could put his mouth to her…

Liyah put a hand over her face and groaned softly. She'd been so wanton. Begging for more. He'd made love to her over and over again. Until they'd been limp with exhaustion and pink trails had coloured the Paris sky outside.

She opened her eyes again. And now it was bright daylight. She felt disorientated. She was not used to sleeping in.

Not used to being ravished.

She lifted her head and looked around. The room was empty. She spread out an arm. The bed beside her was cold. Sharif had probably left hours ago. She felt at a disadvantage. Her skin prickled and she pulled the cover over her naked body, suddenly feeling a little exposed—as if instinctively aware that he'd observed her while she slept.

Now she was being silly. Sharif Marchetti was not a man who lingered over his lovers. His absence was proof of that.

Hating feeling at such a disadvantage, and feeling like a sloth, Liyah got up and grabbed a robe from the back of Sharif's bathroom door. It dwarfed her and it smelled of him. She resisted the urge to hold it up to her face and breathe deep, and gathered up her dress and shoes before creeping back to her own room as if she'd been engaged in some illicit activity.

Sharif watched Liyah from the other side of the room. They were in one of Paris's famous atelier salons, where painstakingly intricate work went into creating the most stunning dresses in the world, primarily for haute couture. Clothes that could literally only be afforded by the very few and very privileged. Clothes that were often likened to pieces of art rather than fashion.

He'd found himself quite unintenionally calling Liyah to see if she wanted to come here with him.

She was wearing a long rust-coloured corduroy dress, with buttons down the front and a brown leather belt. Leather high-heeled boots. Her hair was tied back, showing off that amazing bone structure.

She looked the part of wife of the CEO of the Marchetti Group. Casual, but elegant and stylish. And she was listening intently to an older French woman—one of the typically expert seamstresses who worked behind the scenes to create the astonishing confections that would be worn down a runway at some point in the future.

Growing bored of the conversation he was meant to be listening to, about stats and figures and projections—this kind of very specialised work was at constant risk of being eroded by newer inventions and ways of creating clothes— Sharif gravitated towards Liyah, telling himself that it had nothing to do with the pull he still felt in his blood, that hadn't cooled since last night.

He couldn't remember a night of such unbridled passion. He had been insensible to everything but the woman under him. One orgasm had led to another until he'd been too exhausted to move.

Their night at the oasis had been a mere prelude to the most amazing chemistry he'd ever experienced. And the fact that it was happening with a woman who was his wife…was mindblowing.

Liyah was wearing special gloves to handle a dress, and speaking to the woman in French, exclaiming over the work. The woman was obviously pleased with Liyah's praise, her cheeks pink with pride.

'C'est vraiment incroyable...'

Liyah looked up at Sharif as he came to stand beside her. An electric frisson sizzled up his spine. Her eyes widened as if she felt it too. The buttons at the front of her dress were fastened just low enough for him to see the curve of her breasts, the V in her cleavage.

It was an effort to drag his gaze up and see that Liyah was speaking.

'Martine was telling me that it's taken six months to make this dress.'

Sharif tore his gaze off Liyah and smiled at the woman. 'Your work, as always, is sublime, Martine.'

The woman went even pinker now.

He took Liyah's hand and the hungry beast inside him seemed to calm somewhat. A niggling observation he chose not to investigate.

Just as he was bringing her back to where he'd been talking with the design team at the house, the head designer appeared in their path.

He exclaimed dramatically, 'Who is this creature?' while looking at Liyah.

Sharif felt his hackles rise—which seemed to happen a lot lately, whenever someone looked at Liyah. 'This is my wife, Liyah.'

'You are exquisite.'

The man walked around her, looking her up

and down. She looked slightly bemused. Then he introduced himself to Liyah and took her hand, pressing a kiss to the back of it and bowing theatrically.

Liyah smiled at the dramatics.

Sharif's hackles went even higher.

The designer looked at Sharif. 'I have been looking for the right person to try on one of my newest designs and now I've met her. Please can I borrow your wife for ten minutes?'

Sharif wanted to growl at the man. *No.* But he knew he was being totally irrational. The designer was paying Liyah a huge compliment, and he would look petty if he refused.

'Of course.' He turned to Liyah. 'If you don't mind?'

She looked a little uncertain, but she shrugged. 'Not at all—if it'll fit?'

The designer looked excited as he grabbed Liyah's hand and pulled her away from Sharif. He said, 'Oh, it'll fit—I know it will. And you will look fabulous. Then all we have to do is convince your husband to let you wear it in public.'

The first thing that erupted into Sharif's head when Liyah emerged from behind a curtain some twenty minutes or so later was that there was no way in hell she would ever appear in public wearing the most provocative outfit he'd ever seen.

It was moulded to every dip, hollow and curve

of her body. Being round-necked and long-sleeved didn't make it any more demure.

The designer stood beside him and said in an awed voice, 'Have you ever seen anything more perfect?'

Sharif got out a strangled, 'What is it?'

'A sequinned zebra print catsuit.'

Liyah looked like a feline goddess. Even the fact that she didn't have the confidence of a model couldn't detract from the overall look.

Sharif's phone rang at that moment and he picked it out of his pocket, actually relieved that he had a moment's distraction from the vision in front of him. It was his chief strategic advisor, reminding him of an invitation to go to the opening of a new nightclub in Paris that evening.

Sharif had dismissed the invitation originally, because he loathed nightclubs. But his advisor was saying now, 'I know you don't usually go to events like this, but the club is owned by Felipe Sanchez—who we both know is worth keeping an eye on because he's starting to encroach on our territory…buying up designer labels and luxury brands that are outside our sphere of interest. But, as we know well, today's undesirable brand could become tomorrow's behemoth. We need to keep an eye on him. If you went to the opening, perhaps your presence…and your wife's…would eclipse some of Felipe's bid to grab publicity. I don't think I need to tell you that Princess Aaliyah is attracting a lot of press attention. They want more of her...'

As much as Sharif hated the notion of doing anything in response to someone else's provocation, he knew his advisor was right. The last thing he needed was a rival upsetting his plans before he was ready to unveil them to the world. And, as much as he didn't want anyone else to see Liyah as she was right now, he knew that if she appeared in public in this outfit, on his arm, an eclipse would be guaranteed.

If not a nucelar meltdown...

That evening, central Paris

Liyah was naked in public. Well, not literally naked. But she felt naked—because she was so far out of her comfort zone that it was both terrifying and exhilarating at the same time.

She was wearing the catsuit she'd tried on earlier in the atelier and the material was gossamer-light, heightening her feeling of being exposed. She and Sharif had just stepped out of his car. Before them lay a red carpet, populated by well-known faces from the music world, actors and actresses... And at the other end of the carpet were the glittering lights of the newly opened nightclub. The pounding drum and bass of the music could be felt even from here.

Up till now, attending an event with Sharif had

been a sophisticated and elegant affair. Tonight was something very different. Edgier, younger. Sharif wore a plain black suit and a black shirt, unbuttoned. Liyah saw a girl walk past wearing what looked like two slivers of silver lamé held together by pins.

Suddenly she didn't feel so naked, and when Sharif took her hand and said, 'Okay?' she looked at him and nodded, aware that for the first time she wanted to please him.

When he'd asked if she'd mind wearing this outfit to an event this evening, her first instinct had been to say *No way.* It was the kind of thing she would never wear in a million years. It had been one thing to try it on for the designer—but another entirely to wear it publicly, as if this was the kind of outfit, or event she took in her stride. When underneath it all, in spite of her metamorphosis over the last few whirlwind weeks, she was still just a nerdy academic who loved the outdoors and travelling and learning about the world.

But that wasn't entirely true. Because with Sharif she was discovering that she had a whole other side to her that she'd never explored before. A side that had been shut down after the experience with her first lover in England. A side that revelled in wearing something so provocative even as it terrified her.

Because she knew it had an incendiary effect on Sharif …

After their visit to the atelier he'd accompanied her back to the apartment, and the evidence of just how provocative he'd found the catsuit had had him growling instructions into his phone to clear his schedule before taking Liyah to his room and making love to her with a hunger that had inflamed her. The after-effects lingered in her blood even now.

But now the world exploded in their faces as the wall of paparazzi caught sight of them and en masse trained their lenses on Liyah, in the glittering sequinned catsuit.

A couple of hours later, Liyah was sleepily curled into Sharif's side in the back of the car. to her surprise Sharif had deigned to stay for longer than a nanosecond at the club. He'd even—shock, horror—gone onto the dance floor with her. She smiled to herself at the memory.

Her ears were still ringing slightly after the loud music, so she was only half aware that Sharif was talking to someone on the phone. But then her ears pricked up.

'It worked very well,' he was saying. 'Felipe's reaction alone made it worthwhile attending.' And then, 'There are? Already? Send them to me.'

Sharif terminated the conversation.

Liyah sat up. He was looking at his phone and she saw an image of herself. She looked closer, not feeling sleepy any more. 'Is that me? From tonight?'

Sharif angled the phone towards her. There were a few images of them on the red carpet. And also some grainy ones from inside the club. A rush of hot exposure came back to her as she saw herself straining closer to Sharif on the dance floor, her arms twined around his neck, every point of their bodies touching. She was looking up at him and she looked utterly besotted.

'The pictures from tonight are already going viral. I think it's safe to say that the news of the opening of Felipe Sanchez's new club will fade into insignificance next to the pictures of you in that catsuit.'

'Who is Felipe Sanchez?'

'Someone who needs to be monitored. He's not a threat now, but if unchecked he could become one.'

Liyah felt sick as the evening took on another connotation. 'So he's a rival?'

Sharif said, 'You could describe him as that.'

'And this evening was about deflecting attention from him,' Liyah surmised flatly.

She handed back Sharif's phone and moved away, towards the car door. The rush of betrayal was all too familiar. Along with the sense of exposure. And self-recrimination for having thought for a second that tonight had been some kind of date.

She said, 'I'm under no illusions that this is a

real relationship, but I would appreciate it if you would inform me the next time you're intending to use me as a pawn in your quest for world domination.'

Sharif felt the bite of his conscience. He heard the hurt in Liyah's voice. Impossible not to. And the fact that he was so attuned to another human being, probably for the first time since his mother had died, was an uncomfortable sensation.

She said accusingly, 'That's *my* image that's going to be plastered all over the internet tomorrow.'

'Your image has already caused quite a stir on the internet,' Sharif pointed out.

'Yes, but not while wearing a sequinned zebra print catsuit.'

Sharif felt the distance between them like a physical thing. He didn't like it. He wanted to reach for her, but knew not to.

'You look amazing. That's why you're currently breaking the internet.'

'Maybe I don't want to break the internet.'

Sharif shook his head. 'You have no idea how stunning you are, do you? Who taught you that you weren't beautiful?'

He could see Liyah flinch minutely, and he wanted to curl his hand into a fist and punch someone.

'Tell me again about that guy you were with.'

'He wasn't anyone important.'

'He made you feel insignificant?'

He saw her swallow. When she spoke her voice was husky.

'He was just a guy at my university. As you can imagine, coming from Taraq, I was less… worldly than most other girls my age. He singled me out—made me feel special. I thought he was attractive, but now I can see that I was confused by the attention he was showing me. I was used to standing out because of my height and my colouring. But he seemed to see beyond that.'

'What happened?' Sharif had to curb the violent urge he felt at the thought of such a man uncovering her sensual beauty and not appreciating it.

Liyah shrugged, looked down at her lap. 'He had a bet with his friends that he could get me into bed after one date. I… I was eager to live a modern life. I wanted to lose my virginity, to feel mature, independent…' She looked up. 'He won the bet.'

Sharif emitted a crude Italian swear word in response. He reached for Liyah, unable to resist any longer. She was tense, but she moved closer. She was sinuous under the delicate fabric and he had to curb the urge to rip it from her body there and then. He'd already given in to the storm of lust this bodysuit had unleashed earlier.

'He was an idiot. And he didn't deserve the gift you gave him.'

* * *

Liyah's heart hitched. She didn't doubt Sharif's sincerity.

She couldn't believe she'd told him of her humiliation, but the hurt she'd been feeling upon discovering how he'd manipulated and orchestrated this evening was fading into insignificance next to the way he was looking at her right now.

His hands found where her hair was slicked back into the bun and he undid it, letting it unravel down her back and over her shoulders. He cupped her face in his hands.

'Never let anyone make you feel small, Liyah,' he said. 'You are stunning, and you have a power that I don't think you even recognise fully yet. You're formidable.'

Liyah's heart did more than hitch this time. She quickly tried to negate it. Remind herself who she was with—a man who undoubtedly was a master at complimenting needy lovers. The thought of *lovers* made her want to hiss and spit...

'You don't have to say that.'

'I know,' he said simply. 'But it's true. And if the thought of those pictures really upsets you then I'll have my team take care of removing them.'

Liyah blinked. 'You would do that?'

He nodded. 'I could certainly limit them.'

Liyah asked, 'Will they be good for your business?'

Sharif hesitated for a moment, and then he said, 'In a word? Yes. More than you know.'

'Then it's okay—leave them out there.'

'Are you sure? We have a window to limit this right now, but if we wait till morning it'll be gone.'

Liyah shook her head. She put her hands on Sharif's chest. 'No, it's okay. I know you're not used to answering to anyone. But next time... Just let me know. Okay?'

Sharif's mouth tipped up on one side. 'Deal. Now, will you let me make it up to you?'

'How?'

'Like this...'

He pressed the button to make the privacy screen go up between them and the driver, and then he reached for the zip at the back of the suit, pulling it down so that he could peel the suit over her shoulders, down her arms and away from her chest, exposing her breasts to his hungry gaze.

'Sharif...' Liyah said weakly as he bent forward and cupped one breast.

He looked at her and arched a brow. 'Yes?'

'We shouldn't...not here.'

He blew on her nipple, before flicking out his tongue to taste the hard tip. It hardened even more. Liyah bit her lip.

'Do you want me to stop?'

Never. Liyah was on fire.

She moved back, drawing Sharif with her so he loomed over her supine body. 'No. Don't stop.'

He smiled and it was wicked. 'Your wish, Mrs Marchetti, is my command.'

And even in the midst of Sharif's lovemaking Liyah knew that something had happened here in the back of the car. Something that she didn't want to look at too closely. Because she sensed that, far from renegotiating this marriage as a purely physical thing, they'd moved way beyond that now.

Or, fatally, *she* had.

CHAPTER NINE

Two days later, London

LIYAH LOOKED OUT at a spectacular bird's eye view of London—naturally. Sharif's apartment was the penthouse of one of London's most exclusive hotels. On one side was the Presidential Suite and on the other Sharif's apartment.

Liyah could see the iconic Tower Bridge nearby, and all the way up the Thames to the London Eye.

As per Sharif's schedule, which was emailed to her now, they were here for the engagement party of Sasha and her fiancé. Sasha was Maks's younger sister, but no relation to Sharif or Nikos as she'd had a different father.

Liyah was curious to meet Maks and his wife—and Sasha. And to glean more nuggets of information about Sharif.

She still felt a little tender after Paris. Tender from the revelation that she could no longer ignore.

She'd fallen in love with Sharif. And it had

happened in spite of everything she'd experienced that had made her want to protect herself from such vulnerability. She knew how those who were meant to love you most either left you or just… didn't love you.

It had happened with the speed and impact of an unstoppable train. And she knew why. Because, contrary to that first time, when Liyah had felt 'seen' by her lover, she now knew she had not been. That had been wishful thinking on her part—a need to justify allowing someone the ultimate intimacy. But with Sharif…she really did feel seen.

Literally, in her first interaction with him, she'd been naked.

But it was more than that. She felt an affinity with him that she'd never felt with anyone else. Not even her sister. She saw a kindred spirit in his self-isolation. His lone wolfness. It resonated in her because she'd always been alone too.

Now, for the first time in her life she didn't feel alone.

And it was so dangerous—because for Sharif this was still very much physical. And she sensed that, while her own defences had ultimately been too weak to withstand him, his defences were far stronger.

His life was built around avenging his mother's betrayal and death. He hadn't spelt it out like that, but she'd guessed it. He had a singular ambition and Liyah was a momentary diversion, helping him to that end.

But what of that end? What would happen if and when he did avenge his mother? Would he have peace then? Or move on to the next challenge?

'Ready?'

Liyah turned around, startled out of her reverie. Sharif stood in the doorway to the palatial lounge in a black tuxedo. She sucked in a breath, still not used to the punch to her gut every time she saw him.

'Yes, I'm ready.'

This evening she was wearing a black silk dress. It had a high neck and long sleeves, and fell just below her knee. A gold belt cinched in her waist and the flowing fabric. It was paired with black high heels. She felt covered up and relatively demure, which was welcome after the other night in Paris and the catsuit.

The morning after that night at the club she'd woken to find it torn and in tatters. Much to her mortification. It hadn't survived intact after Sharif's lovemaking in the car, and then when they'd arrived back at the apartment, the zip had got stuck and Sharif had ripped the fabric asunder. Not that Liyah had objected at the time.

But, considering how viral those pictures of her in the suit had gone after that night, Liyah figured the designer had got his value from it. She just prayed he wouldn't ask for its return.

'You've left your hair down,' Sharif commented.

Liyah walked over to him, growing warm from the heated look in his gaze. 'Did you want me to put it up?'

He shook his head and curved a hand around the back of her neck, tugging her towards him. He pressed a swift kiss to her mouth, and even that had Liyah moaning softly. Since the other night, it was as if any restraint was a thing of the past.

They'd even made love on the plane on the way from Paris to London. A flight that had taken less than two hours.

When he touched her like this, or made love to her, it was easy to pretend to herself that it was just physical, but she knew it wasn't. For her.

The engagement party was being held in one of London's most iconic hotels near Hyde Park. When they arrived in the main lobby, Sharif was approached by a man Liyah had never seen before. He introduced the man to her as the Marchetti Group's head of European PR. Liyah smiled, but lost interest as the two men engaged in a conversation about strategy.

She saw an eye-catching modern painting on the wall nearby and wandered over to take a closer look. When she felt a presence close by she looked up with a smile on her face, expecting to see Sharif, but it wasn't Sharif, and it took her a second to place who it was.

The man put out his hand. 'We met in New York, shortly after your wedding. I believe it was your first public event with your husband?'

Liyah instinctively recoiled, remembering the reporter who had confronted Sharif at that first event at the Metropolitan Museum. 'Mr Callaghan, isn't it?'

He smiled unctuously and she recoiled even further.

'Well remembered, Mrs Marchetti.' He took a card out of his pocket and held it towards her. 'I just wanted to give you my contact details, in case you ever feel you want to share what life is like on the inside of the world's most successful—'

The card was plucked out of Callaghan's hand before Liyah could touch it. She breathed a sigh of relief as Sharif pulled her close. His voice was icy.

'Aren't you a little far from home, Callaghan? And this is a private family event.'

The man stepped back and held his hands up in a mock show of humility. 'What can I say? I just happened to be in London at the same time.'

Sharif made a rude sound. 'Clear off, Callaghan. You're not welcome.'

Sharif led Liyah away, and threw the card into a bin as they passed through the lobby. She felt a prickling at the back of her neck, as if the man was still staring after them, but when she looked around he was gone.

In the elevator, Sharif said tightly, 'What did he want?'

'He wanted to give me his contact details. He seems to be looking for a story.'

She looked up at Sharif. His jaw was tight.

'There is no story.'

The elevator doors were opening now, and in a bid to try and move on from that unsettling encounter Liyah asked, 'What does Sasha's fiancé do?'

'His name is Dante Danieli. He's an award-winning photographer and film-maker.'

They stepped into a luxuriously decorated function room at the top of the hotel. Staff came and took their overcoats. Sharif took her hand and led her into the room, which oozed elegant sophistication, dressed in a theme of silver and grey and pink, with huge exotic blooms as centrepieces on the tables.

A waiter approached with a tray of champagne. Sharif took two glasses and handed her one.

Almost immediately Liyah recognised Maggie and Nikos, who had spotted them and were coming over. She was surprised at how pleased she was to see them again, greeting them warrmly.

Maggie said, 'I saw those pictures of you in that one-piece suit and I'm so jealous.' She pointed to her growing belly. 'I don't think I'll ever fit into anything like that ever again. Not that I would even be able to pull it off! You looked amazing.'

Liyah blushed. She felt Sharif's arm come around her waist.

'Didn't she?'

The warm feeling grew as they chatted companionably with Nikos and Maggie, and Liyah noticed that Sharif seemed less tense than he had before.

And then another tall man approached, with a petite woman by his side. He had dark blond colouring. Short hair. Gorgeous. Maks Marchetti.

'Sharif. I see that you're finally having some fun.' He looked at Liyah, smiling, 'And this must be the reason why you've taken that stick out of your—'

'Maks!' his wife exclaimed. She put a hand out to Liyah. 'Hi, I'm Zoe. It's so nice to meet you.'

Liyah shook her hand and Maks winked at her. 'Don't mind me. I just like to wind Sharif up at every opportunity, and it's nice to see him discover he's mortal too.'

Sharif made a rude sound beside her. Liyah shook Maks's hand, momentarily mesmerised by his grey eyes. Very different from Nikos and Sharif. She sneaked a glance between the men as they chatted. Each one as tall and imposing as the other. They packed quite a punch.

Liyah was drawn into a conversation with Maggie and Zoe. It felt quite natural, and she was unable to stay shy for long. They were both so down to earth. Zoe was pregnant too—almost out of her first trimester. She was very attractive, with honey-blonde shoulder-length hair. She had scars on her face that intrigued Liyah, but they didn't detract from her prettiness.

It was more than a little overwhelming to feel as if she was part of this group of people. And then she felt an acute pang as she acknowledged the fact that she wouldn't be part of it for long. She and Sharif would divorce and she wouldn't see them again.

Maks and Zoe excused themselves to go and check on Sasha, who Liyah guessed was the tall woman near the dais. She looked like Maks—a feminine version. Tall. Blonde hair. She was stunning. Wearing a blush-coloured strapless dress. Diamonds sparkled at her throat and wrists, and even from here Liyah could see the huge diamond on her finger.

A man joined Sasha. He was in a tuxedo. Tall and broad. Messy dark hair. He was very masculine, and savagely handsome. He pulled her to his side and whispered something in her ear that made her giggle and blush. She looked happy. Another couple truly in love…?

A dart of envy pierced Liyah before she could stop it. And, suddenly feeling a little too vulnerable to be around Sharif, in case he spotted it, Liyah made her excuses and walked over to where some French doors were partially open. She went outside to the terrace. It was cold, but the first hints of spring on the way could be felt. New life…

London sparkled under the moon. Vibrant and glamorous. It had always been her favourite city. But the desert… That was where her heart lay.

She was so wrapped up in her thoughts she didn't hear Sharif join her, but she felt him when her pulse inexplicably picked up.

'Penny for them?'

She looked at him, so tall and vital and handsome in his tuxedo. She shrugged and looked back out over the view. 'I was just thinking of cities…and the desert. I miss it. I think it's where I feel most at home, even though it can be such an inhospitable place.'

Sharif placed his hands on the terrace wall. 'You miss your horse and your bird?'

She nodded. 'I feel free in the desert. Totally at peace.'

He turned and leant against the terrace wall, facing her. 'When my father sent those mercenaries to kidnap me I blamed the desert for a long time. As if it had somehow betrayed me by not protecting me.' He grimaced. 'Obviously I know better, but that's how the desert is for me—like a living organism.' His mouth quirked. 'I've since forgiven it.'

Liyah said, 'It's so vibrant and full of life, but

it can turn on you in an instant. I got caught in a sandstorm once—scariest experience of my life.'

They stood in silence for a moment.

Then Liyah said, 'I know you said you took on your father's business because it was your due, and your brothers', and because you wanted to make something of it, but I can't imagine it was easy to take over from a man you hated so much.'

'It wasn't,' Sharif admitted. 'I despised it at first. Because I despised him and anything he touched. I thought his business was a vacuous world, full of vain people. I thought it had no value. Until I had access to the accounts and saw the spreadsheets. At first it was very much a means to an end for me—rebuilding it. But over time, as I got to know more, I came to appreciate the industry. I think there's a place for enduring brands in the world. And for fashion and art. We provide something aspirational. Inspirational. And I think we can do a lot of good in changing things for the better. In terms of the environment. Inclusivity. Diversity. Art and design and creativity is what civilises us. If that disappears, or becomes eroded, we lose something very valuable.'

Liyah stayed silent, willing Sharif to continue.

'We had an intern in one of our offices from South Africa. He grew up in poverty in the townships. His mother cleaned in the big rich houses and she used to bring home copies of *Vogue*. For a young gay boy, who literally had nothing else, those magazines were a portal to another world, where he could fantasise about being someone else.'

Sharif looked at Liyah, and pride was visible on his face.

'He won Men's Designer of the Year at the fashion awards a few months ago.'

Liyah smiled. 'I love that story.'

People started clapping and cheering inside.

'We're missing the announcement,' she said. 'We should go back in.'

But Sharif caught her hand and stopped her, pulling her towards him until they were touching. 'I prefer it out here.'

'Do you, now?'

'Yes… I do.

He took off his jacket and placed it over her shoulders, before tugging on it so that she came even closer. Surrounded by his smell and his body heat, Liyah cast aside all her concerns and gave herself up to the moment.

Because she knew that when the time came all she would have to remember would be moments like this.

Later that night—much later—when they returned to the apartment, to Sharif's bedroom, Liyah wasn't prepared for the urgency that gripped her as soon as Sharif put his hands on her face and tipped it up so he could kiss her.

She realised she'd been waiting for this moment all evening.

She was ravenous.

She scrabbled to undo his clothes as his hands moved over her body, undoing her dress, taking it off her. His kisses stole her sanity. She pulled back, dizzy, to see Sharif shed his clothes. A button popped. Liyah felt like giggling, but it was drowned out by the rush of blood to her head when she saw Sharif's magnificent body bared.

He was like a warrior. And she wanted to honour him.

She dropped to her knees in front of him and heard his surprised huff of air. 'Liyah, what are you—?'

But she couldn't resist that straining column of flesh. She wanted to taste him. The very essence of him. She wrapped her hand around him and heard him suck in a breath, whistling through his teeth.

He put his hands on her head, his fingers clamping tight as she inexpertly explored the thick, rigid flesh, running her tongue around the head before putting her mouth around him fully.

Sharif's legs were shaking...his hands trembling. He didn't recognise himself right now, having gone from civilised to carnal beast in about zero to ten seconds. It had taken all his restraint not to leave the party early, drag Liyah back to the apartment like some hormonal schoolboy.

He'd actually fantasised about her doing this, and now he was straining with the effort it took to keep his hips still.

Eventually it became too much. As much as he wanted to find oblivion in Liyah's far too tempting mouth, he wanted to be buried deep inside her more. And that was a revelation he refused to look at now—usually this form of release suited him just fine, feeling like a lesser form of intimacy.

He pulled back and Liyah looked up at him, her eyes unfocused. Her hair was wild and tumbling over her shoulders, almost obscuring her breasts.

Sharif couldn't even speak. He just pulled her up and lifted her, carrying her over to the bed before laying her down. He felt off-centre and, despite the clawing need to plunge deep and find satisfaction right now, he forced himself to go slow, to prove that he hadn't lost it completely.

Liyah was still dizzy from the headiness of what she'd just done, from how it had felt and tasted to have him in her mouth. At her mercy. She'd felt the tension in his hips, the way his hands had trembled in her hair. But now he seemed intent on proving that any notion she might have that she had the upper hand was sadly misplaced.

He came between her legs and pushed them

apart, moving his big hands up to her thighs, spreading them even wider as he bent down, pressing kisses along the tender inner skin, his breath feathering closer and closer to the centre of her body, where her flesh pulsed.

And then he put his mouth on her flesh. She arched her back and grabbed the sheet with both hands, straining to contain the pleasure building at her core. But it was impossible. One flick of his wicked tongue and she was tumbling over the edge, and her body was still contracting when he reared over her and plunged deep, sending her into another spiral of ecstasy, showing her all too comprehensively who was the expert.

Liyah lay there for a long moment afterwards, her skin cooling and her breathing returning to normal. She was shell-shocked all over again at how this was between them. But surely it would begin to fade? This intense need and desire?

She heard Sharif's breathing return to normal beside her. She wondered if he was thinking the same thing.

And then he surprised her by saying abruptly, 'Actually, Callaghan isn't entirely wrong. I do have plans for the Marchetti Group. My plan is to destroy it.'

Callaghan. The reporter who had followed them to London. Liyah turned on her side to face him, shocked. 'What?'

Sharif didn't look at her. 'I'm going to reduce

the Marchetti Group to nothing. That's what I've been working towards. Building it up until it's powerful beyond anything my father could ever have imagined and then selling it off, piece by piece, until his legacy no longer exists. All the success he garnered off the backs of the women he seduced and stole from will be forgotten.'

Liyah went very still. 'But…but all that stuff you told me earlier about appreciating the industry…'

'This won't affect the industry at large. It'll cause a few waves, yes, but the brands will continue to exist. Just not under the Marchetti name.'

'But what if they don't survive without your support?' Liyah thought of the women who worked in the atelier in Paris.

'That's part of my reasoning in making sure we're in a strong position. All the brands and labels will be desirable lucrative concerns.'

Liyah came up on one elbow. 'What about your brothers? They don't know about your plans, do they?'

Sharif threw back the covers and got up from the bed in a fluid movement. He walked over to a set of drawers and pulled out a pair of sweat pants, put them on. They hung low on his hips as he walked over to the window, arms folded.

Liyah sat up, pulling her knees up to her chest. Feeling cold all of a sudden.

Eventually he said, 'No, they don't know.'

'Because you don't trust them?'

He turned around. 'In a word, no. Even if we do have an accord now, I can't say for certain that they wouldn't go against me—and I can't let that happen. Not when I'm so close. They hated our father as much as I did. Nikos's mother committed suicide because of him. Domenico made Maks's and his sister's life hell when their mother had affairs and ultimately divorced him. I still can't trust that they feel the same way I do, but they won't go without recompense. They'll be billionaires, no matter what.'

'You could talk to them,' Liyah suggested. 'Perhaps not telling them everything but sounding them out? They deserve that, don't they?'

She could see the lines of Sharif's body tense.

'They'd suspect in a second. They're not stupid.'

Liyah pulled up the sheet, feeling exposed. 'I think that you're underestimating them. I think you can trust them. Didn't they come into the group when you suggested it after your father died? They've helped you build it up.'

'They've helped you build it up.'

Sharif was so tightly wound that he felt as if he might crack open. Everything Liyah was saying was hitting him in a place that stung. And he had no idea what had compelled him to tell her any of this. It had started coming out of him before he could stop it.

The truth was that on some level he knew she was right. But he'd been alone for so long, living with his plan to grind his father's name and legacy to dust, that the prospect of it not happening was unconscionable. Too much of a risk.

As if reading his mind, Liyah said softly, 'Would you risk putting a rift between you and your brothers for this?'

'Yes,' he answered, swiftly and emphatically. Except this time it felt hollow.

He'd always figured a rift between him and his brothers would be the unfortunate outcome, but in the past couple of years he and Nikos and Maks had gravitated more and more towards one another. It was easier between them now. He felt... affection.

But he slammed down on all that now. Sentimental nonsense. This whole plan would only succeed with the element of surprise. No one could know.

Liyah got out of the bed, naked. She grabbed Sharif's shirt from where it lay on the floor, slipping into it. It fell to her thighs. Her hair was tousled and she looked thoroughly bedded.

She held the edges of the shirt together. 'I'm going to take a shower and go to bed. Goodnight, Sharif.'

Sharif watched as Liyah left the room, an acrid

feeling in his gut. For so long in his life he'd been certain that what he was doing was the right thing. The thing that would finally bring him a sense of vengeance meted out. And then peace.

And yet now all he could see were Liyah's huge eyes, looking at him reproachfully. He could hear her soft voice… *I think you can trust them.*

He turned around to face the window again and cursed. She was making him lose his focus. Damn her. Damn her for not being the wife he'd envisaged—unobtrusive and on the sidelines. Far from that, she was in his bed, under his skin, and every time he looked at her she made his mind go blank with lust.

Damn her for making him want to spill his guts.

And damn her for suddenly making him doubt everything.

Not even a hot shower could warm Liyah up. She wrapped herself in a towelling robe and curled up on the sofa in her bedroom. The extent of Sharif's ambition to avenge his mother and destroy his father even at the risk of alienating his brothers should have shocked her, but it didn't. After all, he'd been prepared to marry a total stranger purely to gain any advantage he could in the run-up to realising his ambition.

She felt cold at the thought of Sharif bearing this heavy, toxic burden for so long. And then she thought if she felt cold, how must *he* feel? He'd been alone for a lot longer than her. Trusting no one.

Obeying an instinct she couldn't ignore, Liyah went back to Sharif's room. He wasn't in bed. And then she heard running water. He was in the shower.

She undid the robe and let it fall to the ground and opened the door. Sharif was standing with his hands on the wall, his head down between his shoulders. There was something so…isolated about his stance that Liyah's heart cracked for him.

She went into the shower and inserted herself between him and the wall. He tensed at first, and those dark eyes with gold around the edges stared at her as if he couldn't believe she was there.

She put her hands on his chest and rose up on her tiptoes, pressing a kiss to his mouth, which was in a hard, flat line. At first he didn't respond. She thought he was going to reject her. But then, as if a dam had burst, Sharif put his arms around her and lifted her up.

She put her legs around him and he leant her back against the wall, running his hand over her breasts, cupping one heavy weight before bending his head to suckle on her eager flesh.

He thrust up into her body, stealing her breath and her soul. It was slow, deliberate torture, as if he was making her pay for extracting a confession he hadn't wanted to make.

Liyah absorbed it all, and afterwards she wrapped her legs around him even tighter, felt him shudder his release into her body.

Manhattan

Sharif sat in the back of his car and pulled out his mobile phone. He texted Liyah.

I'm on my way home.

Then he stopped, deleted 'home' with a scowl and replaced it.

...to the apartment.

The woman was turning his brain to mush. Since that night in London, almost three weeks ago, they hadn't discussed the subject of his plans again. When Liyah had appeared that night in his shower he'd been consumed with so many tangled emotions that he'd almost told her to leave him alone, but then she'd put her hands on him and he'd lost the will to tell her to go.

It was as if she'd sensed what he needed and taken all of him, absorbing his need to exorcise what was inside him.

The following morning, when he'd woken, he'd

felt as close to a sense of peace as he'd ever experienced before in his life.

His phone pinged with a response.

Good for you.

He smiled.

It will be good for me. And for you.

After a couple of seconds:

Promises, promises...

And an eye-roll emoji.

Sharif's blood leapt. He'd make her pay for that. He put his phone away, the smile still on his face.

The past three weeks had been...interesting. He'd had a few events to attend, accompanied by Liyah, and he'd found that as she'd grown more comfortable in his milieu she'd become quite happy to talk to people and not depend on him. If anything, he was the one looking for her now, and he didn't like how used he'd got to having her by his side.

He'd found her in a corner the other evening, talking to a septugenarian professor in Arabic about Taraq.

And one day, at the end of the working day—

for normal people—she'd appeared in his office with tickets that she'd bought for a sold-out Broadway show. At first he'd been inclined to refuse, aware that he had enough work to keep him there for hours. But Liyah had looked so crestfallen that he hadn't had the heart to say no.

Sharif couldn't recall the last time he'd gone to a show that hadn't been a premiere, or part of a gala night. It had been revelatory…how such a regular thing could be so enjoyable. Although in truth he'd got more enjoyment out of watching Liyah enjoy the show. Wearing those glasses that made her look like a sexy academic.

And now he was going home—early, for him—because all day he hadn't been able to get the image of how she'd looked that morning out of his head. Sleepy and sexy. Hair in a wild tangle around her head.

She'd not slept in her own room since they'd returned from London. She shared his room. Which he'd never done with any woman. But he found that he liked seeing her things strewn around the space. Her creams and lotions in the bathroom. Her scent in the air…

He scowled again. He was definitely losing it. The sooner her allure started to fade—as he was sure it would—the better. It was coming closer and closer to the time when he would make the announcement about selling off the Marchetti Group, and he was aware that he was using Liyah as a distraction to avoid thinking about his brothers.

The car pulled up outside the apartment building and Sharif felt his anticipation build as he got nearer to the apartment door. This was also a novelty. Having someone waiting for him. Welcoming him. He'd always been so careful to keep women out of his private space before.

But not Liyah.

As soon as he walked through the door smells assailed him. Smells of Al-Murja. The desert.

He shucked off his jacket and loosened his tie. Explored the apartment, following the smells to the kitchen. He was prepared to see his chef—but it wasn't his chef. It was Liyah. She was wearing jeans and a loose shirt. Bare feet. Hair up in a loose knot.

She was listening to jazz, humming to herself. And the smell of the food made Sharif's mouth water. He smelled spices and lemon. Chicken… Lamb?

He knew he should resist this vision of domesticity. It wasn't what he'd signed up for with this marriage. But it was more seductive than he liked to admit…

Liyah sensed Sharif and whirled around to see him standing in the doorway, leaning against the doorframe. Tie undone, shirt open at the top. Stubbled jaw. Her belly dipped and swooped. Her heart hitched. She felt shy. Which was ridiculous after what they'd done the previous night.

'Hi.'

'You're cooking.'

Liyah smiled. 'I can see why you're CEO—your powers of observation are truly impressive.'

Sharif made a face. He came in, nose twitching. 'What are you cooking?'

'I have a couscous, cherry tomato and herb salad. Lamb and pistachio patties. Harissa chicken. Hummus. Flatbread. Here.'

She handed him some flatbread and hummus. He tasted it.

'That's good. Really good. Where did you learn to cook?'

'I taught myself when I was at university. I felt homesick for Taraq and I found that cooking meals that reminded me of home helped.'

Sharif said, 'I'll have a quick shower and join you.'

Liyah looked at him. 'You're so sure you're invited?'

Sharif came around the ktichen island and pulled her close, covering her mouth with his. She felt the inevitable spark leap to life between them.

Still there. Not gone yet.

With every kiss now, every night of making love, Liyah was more aware that sooner or later there would come a time when Sharif wouldn't look at her in quite the same way. Wouldn't want her with the same desperation she felt.

He let her go and walked out of the room, leaving Liyah dazed and hungry. And, annoyingly, not for the delicious food she'd made.

Later that evening the movie's credits rolled and Sharif looked down to see Liyah curled up on the couch beside him, snoring softly, glasses askew on her face.

He turned off the TV—another first. Although he had a state-of-the-art media centre installed he rarely, if ever, watched anything except maybe the news.

He felt a sense of something he'd never experienced before, and had to take a few seconds to figure out what it was. *Contentment.* A sense of peace. This whole evening had been…easy. Pleasurable.

Normally, when he didn't have a function to attend, he would spend the evening in his study, with a sense of restlessness buzzing under his skin. A restlessness that was now gone.

He made a face. He was losing it. A little home cooking and his brain was scrambled.

He picked Liyah's glasses off her face and put them to one side. He gathered her into his arms and stood up. She made a sound…her eyes opened. Unfocused. Sleepy. *Sexy.*

She burrowed closer into his chest and Sharif's

body reacted to her soft curves. As if he hadn't been in a state of semi-arousal all evening, since he'd returned and found her creating a veritable feast for the tastebuds and senses…

He felt his phone vibrate in his pocket, but by the time he got to the bedroom with Liyah she was awake and wrapping her arms around his neck, pressing open-mouthed kisses to his jaw. He forgot all about checking his phone to see who was looking for him. He had more important things to attend to.

CHAPTER TEN

WHEN LIYAH WOKE UP the following morning she stretched luxuriously, keeping her eyes closed, revelling in the after-effects of Sharif's lovemaking. Blinking blearily, she came up on one elbow and groaned softly when she saw the time on her phone. Nearly midday.

This man had turned her into such a sloth. But it was usually dawn before they were falling asleep, exhausted. Last night had been no different.

A voice from behind her said, 'You're awake.'

Startled, because she'd thought she was alone, Liyah looked over her shoulder to see Sharif at the window. The sun made her squint, but she could see he was fully dressed in a three-piece suit.

She sensed something was wrong and sat up, pulling the sheet to cover her chest, not even sure why she felt instinctively vulnerable all of a sudden.

'Morning… Why aren't you at work?' He was always gone when she woke.

Sharif stepped towards the bed, out of the sunlight. Liyah could see him now and his expression was stony.

'Sharif…what is it?'

He folded his arms. 'Tell me—when do you go into my study to send your messages to Callaghan? When I've left the apartment? Did seeing him in London give you the idea to go to him with the scoop?'

Liyah wanted to shake her head. Sharif was making no sense.

She sat up properly, clutching the sheet. 'What are you talking about?'

'Come and see for yourself.' He stalked out of the room.

Liyah scrambled to find something to wear, pulling on Sharif's robe, which was hanging on the back of the bathroom door. She didn't even know where he had gone, but she heard the sound of the TV and went into the lounge. Where they had been last night… Until she had fallen asleep and woken in Sharif's arms…

Not now.

The TV was on. A news channel. Sharif stood before it, remote in one hand, his other hand in his pocket. She went and stood beside him. And her innards froze when she realised what she was watching.

As if she couldn't make sense of what the reporter was saying, she read the text that ran at the bottom of the screen.

Sharif Marchetti decides to sell the Marchetti Group... Brothers and fellow board members Nikos and Maks Marchetti...unaware of this development... An emergency meeting of the board is due to take place...

The reporter was talking again. 'Only days ago, Marchetti Group shares were at an all-time high. The company had the Midas touch. It could do no wrong. The question on everyone's lips is why on earth would Sharif Marchetti destroy his own company like this?'

Sharif switched off the TV. He faced Liyah, who was in shock.

'Well?'

She looked at him. She found it hard to speak. To articulate anything. 'How...how did they find out?'

'Really? You're really going to pretend it wasn't you? When Callaghan was the one who got the scoop? You met him—right under my nose in London.'

Liyah's brain felt sluggish as she recalled the man approaching her, trying to give her his card. 'Don't be ridiculous, Sharif. Of course I didn't say anything to him. I didn't even take his card. Why would I say anything?'

'Because you disapprove? Because you feel I'm not being fair to my brothers? Maybe you contacted Nikos and he called Callaghan, hoping to cause a bit of chaos so that I wouldn't go through with it. But I think it was because I gave you privileged information and that was an irresistible currency for you. A way to negotiate the end of our marriage well before time so you could get your precious independence early.'

Liyah's legs felt like jelly. She sat down on the chair behind her. 'That's such a twisted theory... I didn't do this, Sharif. I swear. Whatever I felt about your decision, your motives...that's between you and your brothers.'

'Not any more. It's now between me, my brothers and the entire world. Our stock has plummeted.'

'But...wouldn't this have happened anyway, when you made your announcement?'

'No, it would have been controlled. And I was always going to tell Nikos and Maks before I did anything. I just wasn't going to involve them until the last moment.' Sharif looked at his watch. 'I have to go. I have to give a press conference this afternoon and then I'm flying to Paris. I don't know when I'll be back.'

He went to walk out of the room and Liyah stood up. Before he disappeared, she said, 'You really believe it was me?'

Sharif stopped. He turned around. 'You're the

only one who knew the full extent of my plans. I hadn't even revealed them to my own staff. They were kept in a safe in my office, and the only person who has the code is me.'

Liyah felt sick. Sharif walked out. She stared at the empty space for a long moment. Until she heard Sharif speak with Thomas and then the *ping* of the elevator doors.

He was gone.

Liyah was too numb to process what had just happened. She showered, dressed... Sat on the couch in the lounge and watched Sharif give his press conference a couple of hours later, trying to limit the damage.

Thomas enquired if she wanted to eat, but she had no appetite. At some point she went out and walked the streets for blocks and blocks. Always aware of the security man tailing her. She was almost surprised he was still there...

The speed with which Sharif had turned on her, choosing to believe that she could have possibly— Her stomach roiled.

When she finally returned to the apartment it was empty. She slept in her own bed for the first time since that first week she'd arrived in Manhattan.

When she woke at dawn she was gritty-eyed. She checked her phone. No calls, no messages.

Days passed in a hazy blur. Liyah saw news reports about how the board of the Marchetti Group

were holding crisis meetings. She saw pictures of
Nikos and Maks leaving the Paris office, as grim-
looking as Sharif, and her heart ached.

They would hate him for not trusting them.
The damage would be irreparable.

And then, just like a few months ago, when
her sister had called her and begged her for help,
Samara needed Liyah again.

And Liyah saw no reason not to go to her—
because there was nothing for her here any more.

When Sharif arrived back at his Manhattan apartment all was quiet. He knew Liyah wasn't there.
He knew she was in Taraq with her family. Her
sister was getting married within the next fort-
night, sooner than expected. He'd been invited,
but he'd declined.

He shrugged off his jacket and undid his tie.
He went straight to his drinks cabinet and poured
himself a stiff whisky. Not that whisky had done
much to help in the last two weeks since he'd
left. But it had blurred the edges and helped him
forget the dreams that haunted him most nights.
Dreams of *her*. And of treachery.

The liquid burnt its way down his throat. He
poured another. The world was in flames around
him. Everything he'd worked so hard to achieve
was ruined. His father was laughing at him from
his grave. His mother… His heart constricted.
He'd failed her.

And all because he'd lost his focus. He'd let his brain migrate to his pants. He'd forgotten a lifetime of lessons in trusting no one but himself. He'd allowed a siren with huge green eyes to lull him into a false sense of security. To make a fool out of him.

His phone rang in his pocket and he took it out. Saw the name. He smiled mirthlessly and restrained himself from throwing the phone at the window.

He answered it, saying, 'Haven't you done enough damage, Callaghan? Tell me—did you know that first night that my wife would betray my trust? Did she come to you or did you approach her? Actually, I don't even want to know.'

He emitted an expletive and terminated the call, throwing the phone down.

It pinged almost immediately, but Sharif ignored it. He was bone weary.

He walked through his empty apartment, noting that it was exactly how he remembered, before Liyah had arrived.

He walked into her room. There was the slightest hint of her fragrance. But of course—she'd been sharing his room. Because he was the biggest fool on earth.

He went into the dressing room. All the clothes that he'd purchased for her were hanging up. Shoes lined up. Jewellery laid out. He was about to leave when he noticed something and turned back. Her wedding ring. The second one. It was there. She'd never taken it off after he'd put it on her finger. But she'd left it behind.

He should be welcoming the sight of it there. Clearly she'd got the message that the end of this marriage was nigh. But it didn't feel good to see it. He felt as if it was mocking him. For being such a fool.

He turned and walked out, leaving the ring behind.

'You look so beautiful, Sammy—really. Everything will be okay…trust me.'

Liyah's sister was fighting back tears. 'Father threatened to kill him.'

Liyah said in soothing tones, 'Our father is many things, but he is not a murderer.'

Samara had fallen pregnant with her fiancé's baby. Hence the fast-tracked wedding, to mitigate the scandal of sex before marriage.

Liyah said now, 'You're marrying Javid, and that's all that matters. Once you're married our father can't say anything.'

Samara nodded and sniffled. Their other sisters fussed around.

Liyah took a step back for a moment, and saw her own reflection in the mirror. She was dressed in clothing very similar to her wedding day outfit. Traditional Bedouin robes. She quickly blocked out the thought, not welcoming anything that led to thinking about Sharif.

It had been almost a month now, and the pain and sense of betrayal were still acute.

Her sisters were covering Samara's face with the elaborate face veil. Samara put out a hand. 'Liyah?'

Liyah stepped forward, taking her sister's hand. 'I'm right here.'

They started to make the journey from the women's quarters to the throne room, where the wedding would take place. Against her best intentions, Liyah couldn't stop her mind deviating with sickening predictability to Sharif.

When her father had been told he wasn't coming to the wedding, he'd said, 'A husband should be with his wife. What did you do, Liyah? You don't please him?'

She'd actually received an email from Sharif today. But she hadn't opened it yet. She'd thrown away the phone he'd given her, so she had no idea if he'd been trying to contact her via that.

She didn't know what she would do, but she figured she would have to contact him again at some point to discuss the divorce. It was obvious that their marriage couldn't continue now—not when the very reason for her existence as his wife was no longer valid.

His grand plans for revenge had been ruined. And it wasn't as if their relationship was ever going to morph into a real marriage, no matter how hot the sex, or the fact that it had seemed as if Sharif was enjoying spending time with her.

She'd deliberately avoided looking at the international news, not wanting to see the Marchetti Group's demise. Or to see pictures of his brothers again, looking so grim. Had he told them that he blamed Liyah for the leak?

They were in the throne room now, and Liyah focused on her sister. This was what was important. Not her broken heart.

Much later that night, after the first day's festivities had ended, Liyah opened up her laptop. She was tempted to delete the email without opening it, but she was too weak.

There was nothing in the subject line.

She sucked in a breath and opened it.

Liyah, I've been trying to contact you. Please call me. We need to talk. Sharif.

No frills. No elaboration. No doubt he wanted to talk about the divorce.

Liyah typed back.

You can instruct your legal team to send me divorce papers. I am happy to proceed.

And then she sent her reply and shut the laptop. Over the following days Sharif left messages

with her father's aides, but Liyah refused to take
any calls or return them. He sent her more emails,
but she refused to look at them. And then one
day one of her father's aides came to tell her that
Sharif was at the palace to see her.

Liyah panicked. She wasn't ready to deal with
Sharif and his accusations again. Especially not
here, where her father's disapproval permeated
the atmosphere.

She told the aide she would meet Sharif, and
as soon as he left pulled a shawl from her ward-
robe and wrapped it around her shoulders and
head before leaving her room.

A group of female palace workers were head-
ing towards the palace entrance and Liyah followed them, slipping between them. When they
reached the main courtyard Liyah's step faltered.

Sharif was standing beside a four-by-four vehicle in a polo shirt and jeans. Sunglasses. She
wasn't the only one who faltered. Sharif's gaze
tracked to the women and Liyah averted her face
suddenly, hurrying to keep up with them. She
wrapped the shawl over her face to try and dis-
guise herself.

She had no moment of warning, and the breath
left her chest when her arm was taken and she
was whirled around. Dark brown eyes ringed
with gold met panicked green.

'I knew it was you,' Sharif breathed,

He pulled back the shawl, revealing Liyah's

face and hair. Her heart slammed to a stop, before starting again at an accelerated rhythm. She cursed her too-distinctive hair. Of course she hadn't been able to blend in. She never had.

His gaze raked her up and down. 'What are you doing? Trying to avoid me?'

Liyah pulled her arm free, conscious of her less than glamorous outfit. She was wearing a traditional tunic over slim-fitting trousers. Flat sandals. A far cry from the wife he'd moulded to fit into his world.

'I find that I'm not all that keen on being accused of espionage again. I told you to get your legal team to contact me.'

Sharif muttered something under his breath.

Her pulse was hammering and her insides were swooping and fizzing. Even though she hated his guts.

Liar.

She stepped back. 'Just leave me be, Sharif.'

She turned to go, and then he said from behind her, 'I know you didn't do it, Liyah. I'm sorry. I just... Look, can we talk? I need to talk to you.'

Liyah stopped in her tracks. She was breathing as if she'd run a marathon. The other women were gone. She absorbed what Sharif said. *I know you didn't do it.*

Her hurt and sense of betrayal were still acute. And she didn't want him to see that. So she didn't turn around; she kept moving.

Another muttered curse came from behind her and then, before she could react, Sharif was in front of her and bending down. She only knew what he was doing when the world was upended and she realised he'd flung her over his shoulder.

His hand was on her bottom. She was so astounded and indignant that she could hardly breathe, let alone speak.

He opened the back door of his vehicle and put her on the seat. Liyah sprawled inelegantly, looking at him. 'What the hell do you think you're doing?'

His jaw clenched. 'We need to talk.'

He closed the door before she could respond and strode around to the front. Liyah leapt for the door handle but it was locked. Both sides. And then the car was moving.

For a long moment she fumed in the back seat. Sharif was silent. Navigating his way out of the city and into the surrounding desert. Past the oasis. On into the desert. And on. And on. Further and further away. Towards Al-Murja.

Eventually she couldn't stay silent. She leant forward, doing her best to avoid looking at Sharif directly. 'Where are you taking me?'

'It's at least another half an hour. Make yourself comfortable. We'll talk when we get there.'

Liyah sat back and folded her arms over her chest. She caught Sharif's eye in the rearview mirror and pointedly looked away. But she couldn't help but wonder what he wanted if he really did now know she hadn't been the source of the leak.

Roughly half an hour later a structure appeared on the horizon. Despite herself, Liyah leaned forward to look. Gradually it was revealed as a modest fortress-type building, with turrets. Greenery dotted the ground outside. It must have been built on an oasis.

Liyah recognised the skyline of Al-Murja's capital city in the distance. She recognised where they were: the border between Taraq and Al-Murja.

Sharif drove straight up to the building, and to her surprise she saw the gates open to admit them. Her jaw dropped as they drove in. Inside the walls was a lush oasis. Flowers bloomed on almost every wall. Vines twined and tangled around columns. There were ponds and fountains. Palm trees.

The building itself was simple. Two-storey. She could see through it to corridors and columns, to inner courtyards around which she knew would be arranged rooms and quarters.

She wanted to ask *What is this place?* But she didn't want to give Sharif the satisfaction.

He came to a stop in the main courtyard, ringed with vibrant bushes and flowers. It was like an exotic outdoor hothouse. Liyah had never seen so many examples of desert plants in one place. It was magical.

He got out and came around and opened her door. She was tempted to stay put, but the thought of Sharif putting her over his shoulder again made her scramble out.

She looked behind her to see the main gates closing again. A man in a white *thobe* appeared and Sharif gave him the keys to the four-by-four. Then he kept on walking into the building.

With the utmost reluctance, Liyah followed.

Sharif knew she was behind him. He felt her presence in every cell of his body. Regret and self-recrimination burned in his gut. He didn't blame her for being angry. He had betrayed her in the worst way.

The moment he'd seen her trademark unruly hair, barely contained by the shawl, he'd known immediately it was her—as if he wouldn't have guessed from the way she moved. Or her green eyes when she'd looked at him.

He led her into a shaded courtyard, where a table was laid out with refreshments. He turned to face her. She was looking around her. Her body was tense.

'Please, help yourself.'

She looked at the table. And then at him. Folded her arms. 'I don't need anything. Can you just tell me whatever it is that can't be expressed through our legal teams?'

'Did you hear what I said back at the palace? I know you didn't do it.'

'I told you I didn't do it a month ago. You had a choice at the time to believe me or not. It's too late now, Sharif.'

She turned away, but Sharif caught her hand. That physical contact of skin on skin made his body tighten all over.

'Liyah, will you please let me explain...?'

CHAPTER ELEVEN

THE HURT THREATENED to overwhelm her, but Liyah pushed it down, not wanting him to see it.

As if she wasn't that bothered, she turned back, taking her hand from his. 'Fine—knock yourself out.'

She sat down on one of the chairs at the table, crossed her legs. She heard Sharif sigh and sneaked a glance. He was running a hand through his hair. She noticed belatedly that it was longer. And his jaw was stubbled enough to be halfway to a beard. She'd been too angry to notice before now. Too upset. She felt a dart of concern. Then quashed it.

'The truth is that as soon as I was informed of the leak I wanted to believe that you were responsible. I pushed aside any other possibility because I'd trusted you with information that I hadn't shared with anyone else. Not even my brothers, for fear my plans wouldn't proceed as I'd wanted.'

'How did you find out?'

Sharif sighed again. 'I think I always knew in my heart. But it was Callaghan who told me that it was one of my own aides. The man hacked into my safe and copied the documents. News of what I planned was too incendiary to make him resist leaking. He went to Callaghan, my brothers, the board, hoping that by doing so he'd stop the company from breaking up and save his own job in the process, or get promoted to a better position by one of my brothers, in return for the information.'

'How did your brothers react?'

Sharif emitted a caustic laugh. 'How do you think? They were livid. Exactly as you said. But, worse than that, they were hurt. I betrayed their trust badly. And yours. But now we've reached an agreement, and hopefully a solution. We're not dismantling the Marchetti Group. It's going to be rebranded The House of Noor—named after my mother. Dismantling everything my father had built up was always the focus of my revenge. I never really considered the legacy *we'd* built— me and my brothers—since he died. I was too blinkered. But you helped me start to see things differently. I had to acknowledge that my relationship with my brothers had changed. I didn't want to admit that, though, because I didn't want to admit that I cared about them as much as I did. I'm taking my mother's name too—officially. I'll be known by my Al-Murja title from now on. I've left it up to my brothers to decide if they want to hang on to the Marchetti name or not. Maks doesn't care too much. But I know Nikos will probably change his name too.'

A lump formed in Liyah's throat. She hated it that she cared about the fact that he'd managed to fix things with his family. And that he'd managed to honour his mother in such a profound way, by taking her name for himself and the company.

She finally looked at him. 'Why did you blame me if you had a shred of doubt?'

Sharif came and sat down on the other chair. He leant forward, hands linked loosely between his thighs. Liyah averted her gaze, but that was just as bad because she couldn't look away from his eyes.

'Because I realised how close you'd got. How much I'd instinctively trusted you. When I never trusted anyone in my whole life before. Yet within a month of meeting you I'm telling you my innermost secrets and sharing my life with you in a way that crept up on me.'

'I am your wife,' Liyah pointed out with an astringent tone. 'There's a certain amount of trust and cohabitation expected.'

Sharif stood up. Paced back and forth. When he spoke he sounded frustrated. 'I know that. But in my arrogance I believed I could marry someone—anyone—and not have them impact my life in any meaningful way except for the way *I* dictated.' He faced her. 'But then you came along and blew it all up. From that night at the oasis, nothing was the same again.'

And clearly, Liyah thought, not much had changed. He might have realised she was innocent of his accusations, but he still blamed her for upsetting his life.

Liyah stood up too. 'Look…thank you for your apology. You didn't have to go to all this trouble. I know that it's still over.'

Sharif looked at her. 'Over?'

'The marriage.'

Sharif shook his head. 'That's not why I brought you all the way here.'

Liyah's silly heart skipped a beat. 'Then… why?'

He took her hand. 'I want to show you something.'

He tugged her after him and, feeling bemused, she followed. He led her back out to the main courtyard and then around to the side, to the back of the complex. It was huge. With lush greenery blooming from every point. Liyah itched to explore, even amidst the turmoil in her gut.

'What do you think of this place?' Sharif asked.

'It's beautiful. Stunning.' It was like the dream she'd always had of a desert home. Not that she was going to admit that to Sharif…

She could see now that he was leading her to an area of stables and courtyards. More staff milled around. They addressed Sharif as *Sheikh*—Liyah had almost forgotten he was royalty too.

She heard a familiar whinny and stopped. It came again. Half to herself, she said, 'It can't be…'

She let go of Sharif's hand and followed the sound to see her beloved stallion's head poking out over a half-door. She went over, disbelieving until the moment she smelled him, and then she put her hand on his face and felt him nuzzle into her palm, looking for the apple she always brought.

She'd ridden him out from the Taraq palace only two days ago. She saw another stallion poke his head out from a neighbouring stable. Sharif's?

She looked at Sharif, who was standing a few feet away, watching her carefully. 'But…how is Aztec even here?'

'I had him transported yesterday.'

'You…? But why?'

Sharif didn't answer that. He said, 'Sheba is here too.' He pointed to the other side of the yard.

Reluctantly leaving Aztec, Liyah went over to a spacious shed where Sheba was in an enclosed structure far more luxurious and spacious than her home at the Taraq palace.

Liyah was too stunned for a moment to do much but stroke her soft feathers.

Sharif was in the doorway, blocking the light. Liyah turned to face him. 'But…why are they here?'

'Because this is yours, Liyah. I bought this fortress for you, so you'll always have your own home in the desert.'

She was stunned into speechlessness. The emotions his gesture evoked within her were too huge and confusing. Eventually she said, 'But I can't accept. It's too much.'

He was firm. 'It's yours. In your name. To do with what you will. A place where you can come and be free. Independent. Beholden to none.'

Liyah couldn't believe what Sharif was saying. He was literally offering her everything she'd ever thought she wanted and needed to be happy.

But that had been *before*. Before Sharif had come along and blown it all up. Exactly as he'd accused her. Except, for him, it was just a superficial wound.

She shook her head. 'I don't want it, Sharif. It's too much.'

'It's too late.'

Frustration, anger, love and pain all mixed together and threatened to overflow. She pushed past Sharif, moved back into the courtyard, needing air. Space.

'You don't get to do this,' Liyah said through her breaking heart. 'You don't get to buy me a dream castle in the middle of the desert just to salve your conscience so I can be here on my—'

She stopped and turned around, overcome. She felt Sharif close behind her.

'On your what?'

Something gave way inside her. A last defence. She was undone. Reduced to nothing. She had nothing left to lose.

She turned around again, let him see the emotion she was feeling, that was leaking out of her eyes. He went pale. 'On my own, Sharif. I've been on my own my whole life. Until I met you. You made me want more. You made me want things I'd never dared dream I could have. Like a relationship. Even after I'd vowed I would never let myself be so vulnerable. You made me fall in love with you and I'll never forgive you for that. I gave you the power to hurt me—and you did.'

The words hung in the air between them. Sharif didn't move. He didn't turn and get back into the car and disappear as fast as the wind could carry him. He stood there, looking at her with those dark unfathomable eyes.

Liyah couldn't take it any more. She moved to turn away, find somewhere in this vast place where she could lick her wounds, but Sharif said, 'Wait.'

She stopped, but didn't turn around.

He said from behind her, 'Would you forgive me if I said that all those things you mentioned... I want them too? With you. And,' he continued, 'if it's any consolation, I gave you the power to hurt me too. By accusing you of something you didn't do, I pushed you away before you could hurt me. Except it didn't work. Because I hurt myself. And you. And I will never forgive myself for that.'

She turned around. His face was starker than she'd ever seen it.

He said, 'I love you, Liyah. I fell for you as soon as I laid eyes on you that night at the oasis, and I thank whatever serendipitous forces aligned to make you my mystery lover and my bride— because I know that if I had never met you again my life wouldn't have been worth living. I've had nightmares for the past month, and in each one it's our wedding day, and when your face is revealed it's not you. It's a stranger.'

Liyah looked at Sharif. She saw the truth written on his face and in his eyes. Saw the ravages of the past month. She saw them because she felt them too.

She took a step towards him, feeling the fragile, tentative beginnings of something like joy unfurling inside her. 'You really love me?'

He lifted a hand towards her. She saw that it was trembling. But he let it drop, as if he was still afraid to touch her.

'More than you could ever know,' he said. 'And now I know why I avoided it for so long. It's terrifying.'

Liyah took another step closer. Reached for his hand. Intertwined her fingers with his. For the first time in weeks she felt a sense of peace move through her, and also something much more profound. A sense of homecoming.

'I love you, Sharif. And I love this place. But I'll only agree to accept it on one condition.'

'Anything.'

'That you share it with me.'

He reached out, touched her hair reverently. 'I was afraid you wouldn't want that.'

'I do,' Liyah said fervently, moving closer until their bodies touched. 'But I have a question.'

'Anything,' Sharif said again, and smiled.

'If you're no longer Sharif Marchetti, then what does that make me?'

'If you consent to stay my wife then you will revert to your family name—Sheikha Aaliyah Binte Rashad Mansour.'

Liyah bit her lip, feeling emotional. 'Of course I consent. But I think I'd like to take my mother's name and yours—Aaliyah Binte Yasmeena al Nazar.'

Sharif's eyes looked suspiciously shiny. 'I think that is a very fine name.'

Liyah twined her arms around his neck. Desire rose, thick and urgent. 'I have one more very important question…'

Sharif framed her face with his hands. 'Anything,' he said, for a third time.

'Where are the bedrooms?'

'There are about twelve.'

'We only need one.'

He said, 'We should probably check them all, then, to make sure we pick the best one.'

Joy bubbled up and spilled out of Liyah's mouth in a spontaneous laugh as Sharif led her into the building. He turned to her and she could see the fragility of this moment written on his face.

He stopped and cupped her face. 'Is this real? Are you real? Or have I dreamt you up since that night at the oasis?'

If Liyah had had any lingering doubt it was eradicated in that instant. And, just as Sharif had put her hand over his heart that night, to prove he was real, she took his hand now and put it over her heart. 'I'm real. This is real. I love you, Sharif.'

He lowered his head and kissed her with a tenderness and a passion that left her trembling.

When he broke away, Liyah said breathlessly, 'I don't know if I can wait until the first bedroom.'

Sharif smiled and it was full of wickedness, his trademark arrogance returning. 'We're in no rush, are we?'

Liyah smiled. 'No rush at all.'

It was a month before they left the fortress...except for a couple of visits to a very special oasis.

EPILOGUE

Seven years later
Sharif and Liyah's desert fortress on the
borders of Taraq and Al-Murja

'DANIEL, PLEASE DON'T do rabbit ears behind Luna's head this time. Can we just get one photo where we all look relatively normal, please?' Zoe made final adjustments to the camera, which was on a tripod. She pressed a button. 'Okay, everyone—ten seconds. Assume your positions and smile!'

She darted out from behind the camera and went over to where everyone was dutifully gathered in front of a wall of flowers. Maks tucked her into his chest. He stood beside Maggie and Nikos, who were beside Sharif and Liyah.

Nikos was holding a sleepy three-year-old Tessy in his arms—the latest addition to their family—and in front of them were Daniel and Luna, first cousins and as thick as thieves. Then there was Olympia, Daniel's sister, who was holding her four-year-old cousin Ben, Luna's brother, with one hand and four-year-old Stella, Sharif and Liyah's daughter, with the other hand.

Serenity reigned for about seven seconds—until the shutter clicked and children scattered with shrieks and yells, resuming whatever game they'd been playing before Zoe had gathered them all together.

Zoe went over and looked at the camera. She rolled her eyes to heaven even as she couldn't help but smile. 'That's it—I give up. You lot are impossible!'

When Sharif and Liyah looked at the photo later, they laughed. All the kids were making faces, and Daniel was, indeed, making rabbit ears again—this time behind his sister Olympia's head.

Maks was looking down at Zoe indulgently, and she was the only one smiling at the camera. Nikos was kissing Maggie. Sharif was looking at Liyah, who was smiling enigmatically. The fact that he had his hand placed over her abdomen was the first hint of the secret they'd just shared over dinner.

In seven months' time, the Marchetti/Al Nazar/Spiros clan was going to grow by two more little people.

After much congratulations, and tears and hugs and exclamations, Zoe had groaned theatrically.

'Twins? I'm definitely not signing up to take any more family photos. You can find someone else!'

But the next day Sharif and Liyah were due to welcome Sasha, Maks's sister, with her husband and their children. So inevitably another photo would be taken.

The sounds of the happy family gathering had faded into the night by now, and after putting Stella to bed Sharif found his wife standing at the wall of the terrace that wrapped around their bedroom suite—the one they'd spent a very enjoyable month choosing—which looked out over the desert beyond. The night sky was huge, lit up with a crescent moon and bright stars.

Sharif moved behind Liyah, wrapping his arms around her and resting his chin on her head. 'What are you thinking?'

Liyah wrapped her arms around his. Having a family hadn't happened straight away for them. It had taken a couple of years for Liyah to fall pregnant. They'd been about to make investigations when she'd become pregnant with Stella. So they didn't take this latest good news for granted for a second.

Liyah turned in his arms and looped hers around his neck. She wore a short silk nightdress and nothing else, and Sharif could feel every provocative curve. His blood simmered.

'You mean you can't read my mind?' she teased.

Sharif smiled. 'I would never presume to know

what's going on in your head. From the moment I first saw you, you were a mystery, and you still are. You have the power to fell me—as you well know.'

Liyah made a disbelieving sound. And then she touched his jaw, traced the small scar. 'You fell me too—on a regular basis. But, since you want me to spell it out, I'm thinking that I love you, and I love Stella, and I love our extended family so much. I never knew what it was to be part of a loving family. I think I was too scared to admit I wanted one for a long time. We were so happy it felt like tempting fate.'

Sharif said huskily, 'I know.'

She put her hand on her belly. 'I love these babies already, but I'm also terrified because I don't want anything to ever harm them.'

Sharif lifted her hand and pressed a kiss to the centre of her palm. 'No harm will come to them—not from us anyway. And we will love them and protect them until they can fly away and be free to live their own lives. And then they'll come back…with their families.'

Tears sprang into Liyah's eyes. 'I love you so much.'

Sharif shook his head, his eyes shining too. 'Not half as much as I love you. You saved me, Liyah.'

Liyah pressed a kiss to his mouth, and whispered, 'We saved each other.'

'For ever.'

'Yes, my love.'

They turned and went into their bedroom, the vast night around them wrapping them in its protective cloak and echoing the sounds of their love.

* * * * *